parABnormal Magazine
March 2020

Edited by H. David Blalock

Alban Lake Publishing

parABnormal Magazine
Edited by H. David Blalock
Volume 2, Issue 1

First Printing
March 2020

Alban Lake Publishing
P.O. Box 141
Colo, Iowa 50056-0141 USA
e-mail: albanlake@yahoo.com

Visit www.albanlakepublishing.com for online science fiction, fantasy, horror, scifaiku, and more. Stop by our online bookstore at www.irbstore.co for novels, magazines, anthologies, and collections. Support the small, independent press and your First Amendment rights.

A Word from the Editor

As we open a new year, we once again explore the edges of human imagination and understanding in *parABnormal Magazine.*

Of course, you have already seen the beautiful cover art. An impactful and thought-provoking piece by a very talented artist, Scott Lippincott, whose work will more than likely appear again for us.

This time we feature more poetry than usual, with names our regular readers will recognize and some new talent gracing our pages for the first time. Poetry is the expression of image and emotion, the essence of which comprises the substance of the paranormal itself. Our poets examine the very human feelings of fear, insecurity, unease, and curiosity. They look at undeserved punishment and even give us a review in verse of experiencing the phantasms of history.

Our articles this issue have a personal bent as well. From the shade inhabiting the dark corners of a basement to the strangeness that haunts a shelter that should be a haven for battered women and children, we turn to an indepth look at the writing of one of the most famous horror authors of the 20th century.

Finally, the stories. What can I say about the stories? We get hundreds of submissions for each issue and can only publish a few due to budget and space restrictions. We do our best to bring you the cream of the crop. We know not every story will be a favorite for everyone, but we hope to have brought you, the readers, some of the best you will find in any other magazine dedicated to the paranormal.

One thing I have learned in the process of editing this magazine is that the definition of paranormal is different for each person. Its flexibility makes it difficult to determine how to judge a story's adherence to what can be defined as paranormal. Often, it is a bit like trying to catch water in a sieve. The really fine stories may sometimes miss the mark, but that does not take away from their readability. If we had the ability to do so, we would make *parABnormal Magazine* a monthly, even a weekly, to showcase all the talent we run across in the submissions process, but, alas, we cannot. And so, here in these pages, are the best writers we can fit. They are talented, strong story-tellers, with the power to paint a picture in words that thrills, tantalizes, and moves.

I invite you to let us know what you think about the magazine. Drop us a note at parabnormal.magazine@gmail.com. We look forward to hearing from you.

H. David Blalock
January 2020

TABLE OF CONTENTS

The Nobodies In The Crooked House
Gregory L. Norris

The bed constricted beneath him. Colton felt the edges tightening up, closing in on him, hardening beneath his spine. Borders shortened. Space evaporated. Soon, a tiny oblong plot of real estate surrounded his body and was all the world left.

He willed his eyes to open and his lips to form words. At first, he failed.

Wake up, his inner voice screamed.

For a terrible moment, he was flat on his back atop a slab, his whole universe contained within a seven-foot-by-three realm and unable to escape. Then Colton's eyes cooperated, and the living room surfaced from the murk of early morning shadows. He trapped the shriek behind his teeth as it powered up his throat and bolted upright, aware that he was soaked in sour-smelling perspiration. The living room, not that house. It was a bad dream. Only—

He was on their sofa, a lumpy hand-me-down from her cousin's basement. Colton jumped up. The room canted, its ceiling and floor attempting to switch places. Everything turned crooked. He caught himself as he was about to fall and slumped into the rocking chair where she often tried to exorcise her monthlies. He hadn't fallen asleep on the sofa, didn't remember leaving their bed, only her silence after he refused to answer the latest round of questions.

What happened? Were you with Hunter again? You've been acting weird for a week, Colton!

With the room again stabilized, he reached for his smokes and lit up. They weren't supposed to smoke in the apartment, but he'd pulled the battery out of the detector despite the owner's warning it was a crime to do so. Colton had committed worse, the most recent only a week ago.

Bile crept up his throat. The sofa. When in the night had he left their bed? The foul taste of the cigarette added to his building nausea. Colton again stood and hastened down the hallway to the bathroom, one step ahead of his vomit.

It wasn't even seven in the morning. Colton dialed anyway. Three rings, and then he went to Hunter's voice mail. He hung up and redialed, receiving the same deal.

"Yeah, it's me. Call as soon as you get this message. *Later.*"

Colton killed the call. He rinsed his mouth again. Two passes with his toothbrush and an equal number of swishes with mouthwash hadn't killed the taste. Maybe he was stuck with it, as he feared with the rest of what had happened.

She was in the kitchen fixing breakfast. Breakfast on this tense, end-of-summer morning was cold cereal and a banana, which was good, Colton agreed, given what the smell of frying eggs and sausage would have done to his guts.

"Hey," he attempted.

She glanced up but refused to meet his eyes directly. "Hey."

She crunched and slurped. The sound worked on his nerves. Worse, his stomach. He started back in the direction of the bathroom to shower off the clammy sheen of sweat. Like his insides, Colton worried that he'd been marked on the outside by something permanent.

"You're not gonna tell me?" she asked when he was almost in the hallway.

"Tell you what?"

"About what you and Hunter did."

Colton exhaled through his nostrils and turned. "I

told you, we didn't do anything."

He added hand gestures and a kind of dance, not quite hip-hop but in the spectrum, a bunch of peacock moves meant to convince her of his innocence. All lies, Colton knew. And so did she, apparently. Though she said nothing, she wouldn't face him. *Guilty*, her body language answered his.

And he was, like Hunter.

By ten, Hunter still hadn't returned his call, and Colton's nerves tensed for different reasons. What if the law had gotten wise, if Hunter was, at this very instant, sitting in a room full of pigs being interrogated over what had happened a week ago? Every one of Colton's phone calls to Hunter's phone would strengthen their case that Hunter Goudry hadn't acted alone at the crooked house on Farnham Road. Not that he believed Hunter would keep his mouth shut if it came to such a conclusion. If Colton was the one cuffed to the table being grilled, he'd like to think he wouldn't squeal but couldn't fool himself into believing otherwise, even in the thick of hypotheticals.

He dressed in jeans, his old motorcycle boots, a white tank, and his favorite ball cap with its frayed bill.

"I'm going out," he said.

She didn't comment. Absent from the exchange were the usuals—*When are you planning to get a job, Colton? You're not hanging out with him again, are you?* and *He's bad news, and you know it!*

She was right about Hunter but this time she stayed silent, and Colton realized why. Going forward, he was nothing to her. Nobody.

"*They're nobodies,*" Hunter said in his thoughts. "*A couple of skeletons living out on Farnham Road. An easy job.*"

The cigarette dangling from his lips unsmoked

unleashed more of that foul tang across his tongue. Colton spat it out the open window. An unpleasant heat built inside the truck's cab, one that the breeze streaming in did little to alleviate.

All of the jobs with Hunter had been relatively easy. In this part of town, the houses were old as were their occupants. There weren't a lot of security cameras because the homeowners weren't tech-savvy. They kept valuables under mattresses and in jewelry boxes. Easy, sure. The duplex on Cranmore—they'd helped themselves to both sides while the residents were out. The red New Englander on Willow... its occupants, a pair of old men who could have been brothers, roommates, or queers, had boarded the town's blue bus that ferried the elderly or needy to doctor appointments. Over their two-hour safety window, they'd looted over twelve hundred in cash along with another seven in valuables turned around at the pawnshop a few towns away.

Farnham Road had been different.

He drove past Cranmore, Willow, and three other crime scenes, not sure why. But on the ride up Forest, Colton's heart galloped and he knew the reason. A week had passed. The turn to Farnham Road appeared. All the moisture drained from his mouth.

At the last second, he turned. That final, bottled sip of air boiled in his lungs. Breathing was no longer easy or even involuntary. Up a long stretch of green space. Past an overgrown meadow. One old house. Another. More trees.

Hunter's voice continued its invasion of his head, speaking lines from the past that stung at Colton's ear with sharp words. *Yeah, it's safe. Know why I'm sure? The mail, Colton, that's how. The goddamn mail's piling up, spilling over. That means nobody's home—you know how them old corpses set their watches around the mailman visiting six days a week. Well, it looks like no one's brought in the junk mail for about eight—*

The house loomed at his left. At first, Colton couldn't bring himself to face it. He neared, slowed. His truck fell under the tall shadow of the crooked house on

Farnham Road. A noticeable cold that hadn't been there a moment earlier embraced Colton. Slowly, he forced his eyes away from the windshield and over to his left, to the house.

Crooked—that's what his first thought had been on that day one week earlier. A New Englander in the shape of a box, the house leaned like that famous tower somewhere in Italy. This one stood a mere two stories but, even in the bald light of eleven o'clock on a late summer morning, rose up to the height of a skyscraper in Colton's imagination. He choked down a dry swallow, forced his eyes to blink, and turned. The house re-nounced its towering scope but not its crookedness. The place looked ready to collapse right on top of him.

Its weathered exterior was even more timeworn one week after his last visit. The boards of the front porch sagged. Colton remembered crossing them and how they'd shifted and complained beneath his feet—worse than Hunter, who'd flown into a blue streak because he'd used the front door instead of returning through the back. But he'd had to get out of there. Had to breathe fresh air, escape the darkness they'd found inside that crooked house.

His next breath hitched with a sob. Colton's eyes drifted farther back to the metal mailbox fixed to the patch of exterior wall near the front door. Instead of eight days' worth of mail now there were fourteen. The additional six deliveries of circulars and medical bills meant that no one had gone in there. No one knew the truth. Only Colton Van Lundy and his good pal Hunter, who had yet to return his calls.

It meant—

Colton's vomit again attempted to rise. Tears welled in his eyes. Along with bile, a scream powered up his throat. He pushed open the door, leaned down, and cried out as the last of what remained in his guts painted the edge of the sunburned lawn.

***

Nobodies, that's what Hunter called them. Nobodies

who'd had their time and were just clinging on to life. They were no longer somebodies, like the two young twenties alpha males with needs and means.

He'd spied the house while driving through the part of town where old money lived.

"Emphasis on old," Hunter joked while sucking on his coffin nail. "Oh, and on the money, too."

He'd seen the wife, a frail old skeleton who dyed her hair a fine shade of pumpkin-orange, picking through the day's mail delivery. Hunter kept binoculars in his truck for when he lived up to his birth name during deer season. Said he spied an emerald ring on her finger the size of his left nut.

"I know they've got money. Probably have a fortune hidden in a wall safe."

It would be their sixth job together and, by all accounts, their biggest. A bonanz, if Hunter was correct. So far, he had been.

Colton's lady was always riding him to get a job. There'd been a few futile, feeble attempts to please her. When she went through his wallet and found the bills following one of their scores, she froze up, grew distant, rocked in that rocking chair she claimed helped deal with her monthlies. He'd whine for sex, knowing that was the one sure way to thaw her when she went glacial. If whining failed, he'd threaten to leave, find someone else who could keep up with his lust and appreciate all he had to offer. That threat usually worked. Even so, he rued what was ahead, never imagining the many times worse the situation would unfold than he'd predicted.

"The mail?" Colton asked.

Hunter explained. "Which means now's the time to hit those nobodies, because we're somebodies, dude."

***

Hunter parked down the road a ways, in a patch of wild meadow, out of sight. There were no cameras, he said, and Colton believed him. This part of town felt a thousand miles away from the nearest set of electronic eyes.

They snuck through the green belt running behind the neighborhood until the back of the tall, crooked house appeared through the wall of sugar maples and sap pines. The image of the place unleashed a sense of disquiet through Colton's guts, one that grew the closer they got. An old car, one of those gas-guzzling land boats from decades long gone, rusted beside a sagging shed. A length of decaying fence marked what had once been a garden and now was a tangle of weeds and saplings.

"Come on, shake the lead out," Hunter said.

Colton hastened to catch up. They approached the house. Colton forced his eyes higher. The place was crooked, looked ready to tumble down upon them. An unsettled, creaking sound slithered through the air—from branches being stirred in the breeze, no doubt. But on their final approach, Colton pegged it as belonging to the house and its arthritic joists and load-bearing walls.

They scurried up four rickety stairs to the back door. No worry about breaking one of the English panes to force their way in—the door was unlocked, Hunter discovered. Another ribbon of unease flapped through Colton's insides. He told himself it was to be expected, that this was a part of the world where people left their doors open without fear of neighbors breaking in. It was too late to back out of the crime, because Hunter was in the house. Crime committed. Colton followed.

A smell of age and worse struck him the moment he entered the kitchen. It was a big room, with a round antique table and four chairs and old Formica countertops kept mostly clean. Even as his senses revolted, Colton saw the level of orderliness in the place—no dirty dishes in the sink, the dish strainer empty, its contents returned to their proper places, unlike the biohazard masquerading as a kitchen in his own apartment. But a note of bitterness hung over the house, and an unpleasant sound teased Colton's ear, what reminded him of a dog's whimper.

Beyond the kitchen was a hallway and doors leading to other spaces. One, a dining room, contained an oblong table for eight. The glass-front built-ins housed neat rows of stemware, china plates, teacups and saucers, and soup tureens. That's where Hunter lifted the velvet-lined box containing genuine sterling silver flatware.

Hunter handed him the treasure box. Farther along was a soaring staircase, one that ended in a carved Newell post and a few busted spindles. They found the old lady with the rusty bottle job in a broken heap at the bottom of the stairs. She'd taken out those spindles on her plunge downward. One ankle was bent at an impossible angle. A length of sharp bone protruded through her pajama bottoms, which were red with dried blood. Multiple flies buzzed and crawled over the corpse.

Colton turned away and retched.

"Don't do it, dude," Hunter threatened. "Don't mess up this golden opportunity by leaving behind evidence!"

Colton started to correct him—not golden, the chance was *silver*, according to the loot in his grasp. But speaking would make him hurl and so Colton clamped his mouth shut and pulled the neck of his T-shirt over his nose. The impromptu filter helped.

"You check out the rest of the downstairs," Hunter ordered.

Before heading upstairs, where he'd find a thousand in cash in the dead woman's pocketbook, Hunter zeroed in on her finger and that testicle-sized emerald ring. Steeling himself, Hunter liberated it from her bony finger. And Colton thought—*Dude, if that's the size of one of your stones, I'd stop bragging about it!*

Hunter pocketed the ring and hopped up the staircase, taking the steps two at a time. Colton heard him moving about overhead, opening doors and drawers. The dog's whimper resumed.

Colton shuffled forward and tracked it to the front parlor. Half of the room contained old people's furniture—a sofa with a camel's hump in faded pink-red that had clawed feet. The other half was a kind of sick room partially hidden behind a pair of privacy screens. Here was the source of the foul odor drifting through the crooked house.

Cautiously, Colton approached. Between the privacy screens, he glimpsed a hospital bed, a tray table covered in pill bottles, food wrappers, and an overturned water pitcher, and a commode. A frail figure was propped at an awkward angle on the bed. The blankets were soiled. In the space of a second, Colton knew volumes about the situation: the whimpering skeleton was the husband; he was bedridden; the wife, his sole caregiver, had fallen down the stairs to her death, leaving him stranded, uncared for, dying.

The old man's rheumy gaze located Colton. His lips quivered. His mouth opened. What came out was burbled and unintelligible. Even so, Colton understood the plea for help.

Panic seized hold of Colton, freezing him where he stood. Their eyes connected, and Colton's burned from not blinking. An eternity later, Hunter clomped down the stairs. He sighed a swear near Colton's ear. Long last, Colton managed to blink.

"What do we do?" Colton asked.

"What do you mean?"

"Do we call somebody?"

Hunter huffed out a laugh. "Yeah, sure. And then we explain to them what we were doing here when we found the two stiffs."

"He isn't dead," Colton argued.

Hunter ran a look through the privacy screens. "Come on, they're nobodies. Looks like they had a good life together. Now it's our turn."

The other young alpha male strutted away, in the direction of the back door. The skeleton on the hospital bed cried out. Colton's stomach tied itself in knots. He couldn't breathe, couldn't think. The front door—

Doubled over, with tears in his eyes, Colton gazed up. The crooked house loomed hover him. A week had passed. Mail had piled up on the front porch. Surely, left unattended, the old man was now dead. That thought made him puke up his guts once more.

⚡

He drove in a daze, away from the outskirts of town and toward Carriage Hill, where Hunter rented a townhouse from his old man. What they'd done on Farnham Road—worse, what they *hadn't*—followed him like an unwanted second shadow.

The steady chug of heavy vehicles reached him before he saw the lights from an ambulance, one of the town's fire trucks, and the police cruiser, all parked outside Hunter's unit. Colton's heart resumed its gallop.

They'd found out, nailed Hunter—likely because he'd attempted to pawn the dead woman's emerald ring. It was inevitable that they'd come for him next. Probably already were at the apartment waiting to arrest him.

Colton blinked. Ambulance and fire? Those weren't the usual first responder vehicles dispatched to arrest common burglars.

He switched off the ignition and got out.

⚡

Colton entered through the townhouse's back door. A wash of voices and the squawk of radios followed him through Hunter's sty of a kitchen and into the hallway.

"Hello?" he called in advance.

One of the town's finest met him halfway to the front staircase.

"Hold up," the uniform said.

"What's going on?" Colton asked.

The cop's eyebrows knitted together. "Who are you?"

"One of Hunter's friends. Tell me—"

Colton cut past, expecting to be stopped. But he was already at the half-wall and stopped himself from going farther, digging his treads into the timeworn builder-beige carpet.

Hunter's body was sprawled and broken across the staircase landing. One foot in its dirty white crew sock was bent at an impossible angle. As an EMT struggled to spread a sheet over Hunter's rigid corpse, Colton saw that he was wearing the stolen emerald ring on his pinky finger.

*

He walked into the apartment. She wasn't there, and he acknowledged the possibility that she had left for good, had had enough. The rocker was still in their living room, but she'd send one of her friends for it and the rest of her things. It didn't matter.

Colton slumped onto the sofa. The oblong patch of lumpy material became his entire world. He thought about the old man in the crooked house on Farnham Road confined to his hospital bed, abandoned and left to die.

At one point on that long, lonely night, Colton caught himself whimpering like a dog to the empty room.

The Herd Lord
Beth H

Herd Lord by Beth Hudson

Dark times find the esch peoples encroaching on centaur lands. The Herd Lord, Iffrix, sees no choice for the centaurs but to defend themselves and their lands, and issues a call to arms. Left in charge, his wife Niesha expects nothing more than to keep the country running with the help of her allies. But when blue wolves attack, she must deal with dangers of her own to protect her people and make sure there is a country for the stallions to return to. But the larger question remains: is there a traitor within their ranks?

Beth Hudson's novella of the ones left behind leaves the reader on the edge of the seat, hoping against hope, but still wondering, for all of that, whether it is possible to save the centaur people.

Available at www.irbstore.co
Or use the order form at the back of this book!

Hunter's Visitant
Scott J. Couturier

Baying hounds howl at Hunter's bright moonrise—
frost fells flowers & fletches window-panes.
Stasis of Autumn's drowse as firelight writhes,
chill wind wafting leafy specters down lanes.
At length, the queer quiet of home & hearth
becomes a strain of silence, boding ill—
inchoate wraiths flit by on darkened garth
as night-time waxes fey with Witch's will.
Again, that howl! Now, a scratching is heard
at window's ledge, as of talons grasping.
The mind riled by apprehensions absurd—
in the hall! *Something* groaning & gasping!

Just then the candle via draught is out-blown—
by macabre moonlight my grim visitant shown.

The Dawn
Jasmine Arch

Moira comes here when she needs to get away from him. It's always been her favourite spot. The sun appears between the trees and reflects their slim trunks in the perfect stillness of the stream. She loves the light here, no matter what shape it takes. It's as precious in the freshness of dawn as in the wildness of a storm.

This place almost turns her back into the girl she used to be. The girl who fell in love with the wrong boy and allowed him to break her.

Today, the light is unlike anything she's ever seen: ethereal—delicate and indestructible at the same time. It burns behind her eyes to the rhythm of her pounding head, but she can't look away.

The scent of crushed grass beneath her feet smells fresh—clean—but the stench of his sweat and stench of the liquor on his breath still cling to her dress.

The sunlight chases the chill from her aching bones. As she smiles, the cut in her lip stings and begins to bleed again. The pain doesn't matter, though. The sun drives off the cold that's always there—the fear of him.

She walks along the stream, towards the rising sun and the riot of dawn colours that fills the lightening sky.

A hole catches her foot and she falls, twisting her ankle and driving needle-sharp pain through her already-pounding head. Rising to her feet and ignoring the increasing dizziness, she barely limps. Hiding her injuries has become second nature. As she walks on, her pain slowly fades.

The world spins around her as she stumbles and falls a second time. Everything goes black.

When she opens her eyes, the pain has gone.

A man stands before her, features hidden in shadow. He can hide his face but his voice—

She'd know it anywhere.

"Look what you made me do! You useless whore." His words echo through the wide open space. "And now you're leaving me? You're nothing without me."

"I'm not nothing. I never was." Moira pushes herself up, sitting on her knees.

The shadow steps forward. "So you really are going this time."

"Yes. I can't take it anymore. I won't." Rising with all the grace she once possessed, she clenches her fists and stares him down.

"Don't go. It was an accident. You know it was." One hand reaching for her, he takes another step. "Please, Baby. It'll never happen again. I promise."

"And how many times have you made promises, only to break them?"

The shadows around him melt away and brown eyes look into hers as gentle hands caress her cheeks. "It'll be different this time." Warm breath fans her face as he leans in to kiss her.

"I don't believe you." She plants her hands against his chest and pushes him away.

"I'm sorry, honey. I'm so, so sorry." He falls to his knees, clinging to her. "Please don't leave me, baby. Please. I love you. I love you so much."

The hint of a smile graces her lips at older memories. Memories of a different man. Thoughtful and romantic, with eyes that could melt her insides and make her clench her thighs together with nothing more than the prelude to a kiss.

He owned her in that magical moment when the nearness of his lips burned on hers with more intensity than any true touch ever could.

He owned her in the years that followed. Years full of fists, tears of regret, and broken promises.

She pulls her hands free, shaking her head. "I'm not coming back. I can't. You don't control me anymore."

The wind picks up and he fades, blown away in a wisp of smoke.

Finally free, Moira walks forward, never looking

back to the broken body she left behind.

After years of terror and pain, his ownership has ended. She walks towards the sunlight to find freedom—peace.

She feels lighter and lighter, as if the sunlight lifts her. When she raises a weightless arm, light shines through it, turning it a delicate shade of pink.

Moira looks back one last time at the battered shell lying amid pearls of dew. A bruised face stares up into the sky with a smile on its cracked lips.

Unwilling to resist the call of the light, she turns away and runs forward into the dawn.

A Scary Shelter
Luisa Kay Reyes

When my colleague and I were in our final training session to work as shelter supervisors at a domestic violence shelter for abused women and their children, I asked the head lady what the shelter was like, for I had yet to tour the actual building where the shelter was housed.

"Scary," responded my colleague, unhesitatingly.

"Nice and cozy. Very homey," stated the top boss as quickly as she could.

My colleague was right. For as soon as we entered the brick house that had seen its better days long before, I was immediately overtaken by a strong sense of eeriness that the dimly lit dwelling exuded. And no matter how hard I tried to convince myself that the spooky aspect was the result of an overactive imagination, creepiness simply emanated from every nook and cranny in the house all the way from the attic to the basement. Yet despite this ominous nature of the shelter being overtly obvious to all of us shelter workers, the nonprofit organization viewed and boasted of it as a source of pride.

The shelter had been donated to the nonprofit organization and it was the only refuge in the area for victims of domestic violence. Finding myself unable to argue against such benevolence, I dismissed my initial impression of the sinister dwelling, and proceeded to learn all of the procedures for handling crisis calls, the housekeeping chores for which we were responsible, and all of the rules about whom to admit into the shelter and when.

Much to our surprise, the first new client intake my colleague and I did was for a lady who was so proud about being the daughter of a university professor, she felt that listening to the house rules while we read them to her was far beneath her intellectual capability. But through much patience and insistence, we finally spoon fed them to her in spite of her pronounced reticence only to have her end up causing a fury during the night by tearing up her room, thinking she had seen her ex-husband come in. In her frenzied state she accomplished superhuman feats such as pulling out solidly built clocks from the wall in her attempts to thwart this ex-husband of hers. This was so frightening to all of the other clients in the shelter to such a degree, that within a few days she left to join a nunnery only to have the convent ban her from it within a few days.

The rule when we were hired was that each shelter worker had to supervise the shelter solo for a full weekend. There was a requirement that we were to sleep in a locked room in the basement that included two small beds. Yet, it quickly became known among us employees that all of the workers were leaving it unused, quickly taking their bedding up into the living room or to the front office to try and catch some shuteye there as soon as the bosses left for the day.

However, when my turn came to do the weekend shift, I was determined to follow the established procedures of the shelter. So even after the bosses left, I kept my bedding in the locked room in the basement. After a full day on the first weekend I was on duty, I checked the alarm systems and made sure every single one of the doors was firmly bolted and locked. Feeling relieved when all was quiet at last, I finally lay my head down to sleep.

The quietness was short-lived. For very soon, I felt the entire room shaking and the sound of crying coming from the room next door. The two clients in that room had seemed so content earlier in the day that it astonished me to be hearing the sounds of sobbing coming from their direction. Tossing my brief foray into the world of sleep to the side, I quickly got up and decided to see what was the matter. I found to my astonishment that one of the clients was in convulsions. She was trembling and weeping uncontrollably. We had been trained on issues related to date rape and domestic abuse, but convulsions were not something that was ever mentioned in any of the literature or videos we trained by. Perplexed as to what to do, I asked her how I could help. This very much caught her by surprise and for the briefest of moments, her convulsing and sobbing stopped while she stared at me in disbelief.

Then she went right back to trembling and shaking the entire building - just as before. Seeing that my attempts at consoling her were futile, I went back to the locked room and gathered together some of the highly sought after shampoos and body lotions that the women loved so much. Even victims of domestic violence still appreciate the femininity of beauty products. These gifts which she gratefully accepted only to have the convulsions continue, but with the dawn of morning, while the rest of us were trying to recover some of the lost sleep we had suffered during the night, she was the first one to awaken all cheerful and smiling as though she had not a care in the world. She wasted little time in demanding that I let her out for the day.

It took me a while before I put two and two together, but I did finally realize drugs were at play. However, since the shelter didn't test for drugs, due to the fact that a lot of women turn to them to emotionally escape from the trauma of abuse, my hands were very much tied in that regard. I then spent the rest of the morning letting out all of the clients one by one as they left for the day on that sunny Saturday. I noticed when I walked past the dimly lit dining room that the chair at the end had been pulled out. It seemed strange since we hadn't used it that morning, but I simply pushed it back into place.

About midday, I was so overcome by exhaustion from the many cleaning related chores I had to do and the previous sleepless night, that I took a cue from my colleagues and lay down on the sofa in the living room to rest my eyes, forsaking the room reserved for us downstairs. However, no sooner had I closed my eyes, when my nose was met with the strong smell of smoke.

"*Oh no! The shelter is on fire!*" I thought to myself, springing up and rushing to the kitchen and every room in the shelter.

But I soon realized that not a thing was out of place in any of the rooms. Yet I couldn't escape the heavy scent of smoke no matter where I went in the shelter. I couldn't see it, but the smell was unmistakable. I finally looked up at the smoke detectors in the living room and realized that not a single one of the many alarms we had in every room in the shelter had gone off.

This puzzled me, as we were very meticulous about making sure the batteries weren't dead. So I checked the lights and as expected, they all appeared to be fine. Not knowing where else to look, I glanced outside and saw that some of the college students next door were having a cookout. I was struck by the fact that the smell of smoke coming from their grill wasn't the same as what I inhaled inside the house, but it was the only rational explanation that manifested itself. So, in my weekend report, I included that the fire alarms were not going off and needed to be checked.

After the scent of smoke started dissipating, I again walked past the dining room table only to find that the chair at the end was pulled out once more. I figured my clothing must have caught on it during my mad rush to check for any signs of a fire, so I pushed it back into place, wondering a little bit about the peculiarity of it.

That evening, while I made my rounds to check that the doors were all firmly bolted shut and I could safely set the security alarm for the night, the dark shadow of a man rapidly running past me flickered quickly in my eyes. I blinked. That simply couldn't be. It must be that my eyes were playing tricks on me. I double-checked to make sure the doors were indeed firmly locked, for the biggest fear that we took great measures to protect against, was that one of these abusive ex-boyfriends would come seek revenge at the shelter. Blinking my eyes over and over again to make sure they were okay, it dawned upon me suddenly that I had kept the doors locked all day and I had been alone in the shelter all afternoon. There simply couldn't be a man inside unawares. And he certainly couldn't have run out of the door and bolted it tightly behind him. But, I had seen his shadow. So I went to the front office and called the police, asking them to come do a welfare check to make sure no one was lurking about. A request which they graciously obliged, only to find no one.

Once more when I walked past the dining room table, the chair at the end was pulled out. Still a little bit shaken up by the shadow of the man running, this time I simply decided to let it be. After all, the bosses wouldn't come until the weekend was over.

At the end of the weekend, when I turned in my report, my bosses merely stared at me. It had been a rough weekend and some of the clients felt I hadn't done enough to protect them from the drug-addicted client. So I attributed their rather solemn reactions to that and, shrugging off their stares, I gathered my belongings and went home to catch up on some much needed rest.

A few days later, another colleague of mine called me most upset that she was in the shelter all alone with no clients. After my weekend trying to keep everyone safe from the convulsing client, I asked her "But don't you think it is better that way?" A question to which she didn't respond. She abruptly told me she had to go, but she did call me back later that evening with the explanation that she had also called her sister in-between and I got the impression that she'd keep calling me all night.

Finally she told me "The ghosts here don't like the shelter workers and they try to run everybody off." I hesitated. I respected my colleague, but I sure didn't know how to respond to such a statement. Then she proceeded to tell me that there was "a little girl who likes to sit at the end of the dining room table" and a light-bulb flashed brightly inside of my head. *That explains why the chair was always pulled out!* I thought to myself.

My colleague then further related to me that some of

the workers had seen an older Italian looking lady. The smoke was a common occurrence and almost all of them had seen the man running quickly past them, with many concluding that he must be the one who had set the fire. By this point, everybody reasoned that there must really have been an inferno in the building at one point in time.

Startled by her enlightening revelations, I decided to disclose to my colleague my experiences from my first weekend manning the shelter solo, leaving her completely stunned. Unbeknownst to me, my colleagues had concluded I'd be too sophisticated to share in these inexplicable occurrences, resulting in my being the last one to know about all of these shared paranormal observations. I suddenly found myself wondering if I hadn't squeezed the poor little girl "to death" every time I pushed the chair back in. I also began pondering if that first new client of ours had really seen something during her pulling-things-out-of-the-wall frenzy, after all. Mental illness was very frequently present in our clients, but maybe in this instance she had actually spotted something quasi-real.

Lastly, my colleague and I concluded that the owners of the house must have donated it to the nonprofit organization for the tax write off, since with such a heavy amount of paranormal activity going on, they would have had a most difficult time selling it. It was quite a modern day twist on the white elephant gift. All I could do was keep talking to my colleague and hope and pray the ghosts would spare her from their fiery fate.

a message from beyond
R Jean Bell

for months she whispered
in your dreams
but you didn't realize

then for valentine's day
she made her plants bloom
the last ones she'd ever bought
you fought to keep alive

only you blamed the weather
so unseasonably warm

finally she got her chance
and appeared beside your bed
translucent and glowing
she clung a moment
to the bedpost

you thought at first
that you were crazy
but at last
you understood

after all those times you traveled
when she'd had you call when you arrived
she couldn't leave you home alone
without making sure you knew
she was safe there
on the other side

The Hall Of Portraits
Derek Muk

Victoria's heart began racing, *kaboom, kaboom, kaboom,* and beads of perspiration lined across her brow. She felt herself slowly losing consciousness, getting lightheaded. It always happened when she laid eyes on the framed oil portrait sitting on the easel for too long, the one showcased prominently in the window display of the gallery. She wondered if it had the same effect on other people.

She approached the artwork now, cautious, as if she were walking towards a growling pit bull dog that she had to go past on the sidewalk. Dreading this moment. When she was within five yards of it, Victoria finally raised her head and looked up at it, as if seeing it for the first time.

Depicted within the confines of that golden frame was a medieval castle and more specifically, the main wooden doors of it, which had been thrown wide open. A group of people were walking, no *hobbling* out past those doors. One figure was drawn and rendered larger than the others, being in the forefront of the painting, and the first one out the door.

Victoria cringed when she saw the mass of boils and scars on the man's face, at the discolored pus oozing out of those holes, and at the sheer look of desperation and gloom on his face, clothed in nothing but a bunch of soiled and filthy rags. Hair all disheveled and sticking up. She wrinkled her nose, almost smelling that incredibly foul odor on what was probably a typically humid day in Europe, and could *feel* herself in this man's shoes and felt his plight as well. On a day when he probably died. Such a horrible visage and situation to feature in a piece of art. Yet it was here, right there before her eyes. And she had customers who would happily shell out big bucks for an item such as this without batting their eyelashes and hang it above their fireplace.

But what do I know? She wasn't an art snob or critic. But she did like art and appreciated it for what it was. During her upbringing in one of the most notorious ghettos in Richmond, her family did not expose her to such fine things in life but that certainly wasn't their fault by any means. They had other things to worry about, mainly day to day survival. Now Victoria was making ends meet by working in a posh gallery in an affluent white neighborhood in Walnut Creek. Go figure. She never expected to wind up being employed in an establishment like this but you do what you got to do to survive. You had to put bacon on the table somehow and this is how Victoria managed it and she was doing it fairly well so far, knock on wood.

When her heart began pumping faster and she felt the first droplets of sweat forming on her forehead. She turned away from the artwork. She strode over to her faux marble desk sitting in the front of the gallery, picking up a bundled batch of mail, secured by a rubber band. After unstrapping the band, she began sifting through the fat collection of correspondence. Nothing but bills and garbage this week, customer orders, sweepstakes notices, and junk mail circulars. What a waste of paper. Poor old trees.

She sat in the chair behind her desk, slicing open the envelopes containing the orders. Ahh, yes, the payment from Mr. Perez. *Finally! It was about time.* She'd been waiting for his check for weeks, wondering whether he was vacillating between purchasing the painting or not, or had decided to forget about it altogether. Most of her customers were solid and followed through when they said they wanted a particular item. So, good for Mr. Perez! *Yoo-hoo!*

Victoria held the check in her hand, regarding it for a moment, as if savoring victory that had eluded her for a long time. She stashed it away in a steel cash box in one of her drawers, along with some other checks, before plowing through the remaining customer orders.

The phone on her desk rang as she was going

through the other checks.

She picked it up after the third ring. "Good afternoon, Olson Galleria, how can I help you?"

"*Ah, Victoria!*" a man burst out. "Great to hear your voice! Glad I caught you in person rather than your dreaded voice mail this time. This is Hal Perez."

"Hello, Mr. Perez." All professional and neutral.

"Can I pick up my painting today?"

She turned her head to glance at the painting. "You sure can." Her heartbeat had returned to normal, thank God. No more weird stuff. "Thank you for your check."

"When I first laid my eyes on that painting I already knew it was mine. It was sheer gut instinct. Know what I mean? No *ifs, ands, or buts.*"

Victoria craned her head back to look at the painting again, wondering what in heaven's name he possibly saw in the thing. But oh, well. To each his own. Or *her* own. Who was she to judge? She was simply the lowly shopkeeper here.

"When would you like to pick it up?"

"Around two. Does that work for you?"

"That sounds great. See you then, Mr. Perez."

"Oh, please call me Hal, *dear.*" Like they were best buds from back in the day, which they certainly were *not.*

⌁

Hal Perez jerked his head back from the driver's seat of the car to admire his precious treasure of artwork, reassuring himself that it was still there. Yep, there it was. Wrapped up nice and snug under brown butcher paper in the backseat. No way was anyone going to get his painting. No fricking way! He paid for it and *owned* it now. It was his find, his baby now. The only way anybody was going to get a hold of it was over his cold, dead body. But fat chance of that happening.

He stopped at a red light, turning his head around to inspect it once more, an excited grin etched on his dark-skinned face. *Blam! Blam!* Two angry honks from the motorist behind him woke him up out of his revelry and daydreaming. He waved his hand up in the air apologetically to the driver and stepped on the gas.

Oh, he could admire it until the skies fell. He had spent weeks trying to decide just where to display this latest addition to his collection and he had found the perfect place for it.

Fifteen minutes later, he pulled into the driveway of his house. He got out of the car and gingerly brought the painting out from the backseat, placing it down horizontally on a flat bed dolly. He carted the painting inside his dimly lit home, his man cave, curtains all drawn to protect his collection from prying, greedy eyes, crammed full of weird little objects, movie memorabilia, and one of his passions, his ever growing army of art.

Hal pushed the dolly down a narrow, claustrophobic hallway, vintage movie posters adorning the walls on both sides. A prop sword, shield, and helmet from the 1981 fantasy movie, *Clash of the Titans*, were just a few items displayed behind a nearby glass cabinet. Featured prominently on Styrofoam heads in another cabinet were three ape masks, that of a chimpanzee, gorilla, and an orangutan, used in the original *Planet of the Apes* film from 1968. At the end of the hallway was a male mannequin who donned the red Visitor uniform, dark sunglasses, and cap from the 1980s science fiction TV series, *V*.

Hal pushed the dolly into the living room, with every corner and crevice seemingly filled with esoteric artwork of some kind. Everything from actual, touched-up human skulls on the mantel of his fireplace, glass jars full of what appeared to be small human fetuses, to tiny shrunken heads of an indigenous tribe. He quickly stepped over to the main window and opened the curtains just a tad so that some natural yellow sunlight could illuminate the room and give it some vibrancy and life and make it appear less like a dungeon.

Hal carefully lifted the artwork, removing the brown butcher paper, and hung it on two hooks on the wall above his hi-fi entertainment center. He stepped back to make sure it wasn't crooked. *Perfect!* he thought.

Centered beautifully. The sunlight showering in really brought it to life. He thought he saw the surface of the painting ripple a little, barely noticeable if he had blinked, then he saw it breathe up and down, exactly like a human chest would do. *Up and down.* He had witnessed that, no question about it. *Nice and easy, buddy.* Hal blinked his eyes fast to make sure he wasn't imagining it. The painting remained perfectly still. *Whoa, wait, I just saw it move! I swear to God, on my dead mother's grave! Sorry, Mom!* But nothing else happened.

It must be all the excitement and giddiness. It was getting to him and affecting his senses and perception. *Yeah, that was it. Just calm down, dude, and everything will be fine. Relax and chill.* And he intended to do just that, striding straight to the kitchen, opening the window wider to get some fresh air, before pouring himself a shot of his finest whiskey. He gulped it down and walked back to the painting, studying it like an art critic would do at a fancy gala reception in a chic gallery in New York City.

Minutes passed. *Tick tock, tick tock.* Hal generously poured himself another shot, splashing some on the counter, downing it, before he headed back to the painting and gazed at his prized gem once more. His precious trophy hanging in all its glory and beauty.

Several more minutes passed... the more he kept staring at the painting, the more he realized that his heartbeat was now fluttering like a hummingbird's, faster and faster, accelerating, about to reach a crescendo it seemed. Beads of sweat trickled down his forehead, yet it wasn't warm at all. Something didn't feel right. He didn't feel like his usual self.

Maybe it was the booze...

Suddenly, the surface of the oil painting gradually swelled out, to an almost freakishly grotesque level, like a human lung sac expanding to take in oxygen. The sunlight spotlighted the painting and enhanced the surreal spectacle even more. The canvas rose up and down like a human chest would do when breathing. It was like something out of a Salvador Dali work.

Up and down! Up and down!

Hal blinked his eyes again to make sure he wasn't hallucinating. But when the surface of the canvas continued rising up and down like a living, breathing being, his jaw dropped open at what he was witnessing.

"What the hell!" he muttered, feeling his heartbeat increasing further, to the point where it felt like it would literally rip out of his chest. By now, he was sweating bullets, his entire face completely wet now.

The more and more he looked at the artwork, the further he grew obsessed with it, and the more *it* drew him closer to it, like a magnet. His feet shuffled forward, going towards it. He had absolutely no control of himself anymore, feeling like a marionette. Hal couldn't stop looking at the painting. It was like a super addictive drug, making him crave it more and more. No matter how hard he tried, he simply couldn't turn away.

"What's happening?!" Hal asked the silence, not able to move his limbs at all, and not able to break out of this vise-like death grip he was trapped in. He was basically paralyzed.

Panic raced through his mind. How was he going to get himself free?

But his eyes remained transfixed on the painting, at the man with the hideous boils on his face. Soon, Hal was within arm's length of it, and seconds after that, he was literally being *sucked* into the painting. There was a brief sound, *whoosh*, and his legs were dangling out of the canvas, with his feet being the last part of his body to be swallowed whole.

Seconds later, the surface of the portrait seamlessly sealed itself back up, as if nothing had occurred at all. The surface smooth like before.

Hal uttered a scream but it fell upon deaf ears.

Moments passed before he realized he was lying curled on the ground in a fetal position. *Am I still alive?* He wasn't sure, slowly moving his arms and legs around, stretching his fingers out, to confirm if he was really alive or not. He could move! His body was not paralyzed anymore. Good.

Hal moved into a sitting position, looking around him. *What the hell?!* After the smoke had cleared, he discovered himself sitting on a cobble-stoned path, and as he turned his head to look behind him he saw the open doorway of a medieval castle. People wearing filthy robes, with dark lumps all over their faces, hobbled towards him. Desperation and death in their eyes. They reached out to grab him.

Hal immediately got up but felt woozy, his head spinning with a splitting migraine headache. Pale green vomit sprayed out of his mouth as the world spun round and round. Fortunately, he maintained balance on his feet and tried to run, but the plague-ridden group seized him with hungry fists and pummeled him back down to the cobble-stoned ground.

When Hal's hand touched his own face in the scuffle, he felt huge boils, scars, and pus oozing down his face. *What the... I'm in the painting now! How the heck did that happen?* His fingers dripped wet with the liquid. *Holy crap!* When he looked down he noticed he was clothed in soiled rags himself, wrinkling his nose at the fetid odor before puking again.

He tried to fight back but the group overpowered him. Their long, sharp fingernails clawed the skin on his already ruined face and blood splattered to the floor. Before Hal realized it his fragile face fell apart and collapsed to the ground with a squishy thud.

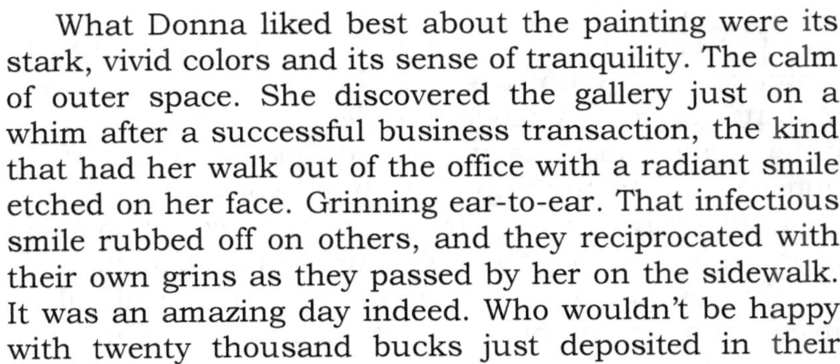

What Donna liked best about the painting were its stark, vivid colors and its sense of tranquility. The calm of outer space. She discovered the gallery just on a whim after a successful business transaction, the kind that had her walk out of the office with a radiant smile etched on her face. Grinning ear-to-ear. That infectious smile rubbed off on others, and they reciprocated with their own grins as they passed by her on the sidewalk. It was an amazing day indeed. Who wouldn't be happy with twenty thousand bucks just deposited in their bank account? When someone told you money wasn't everything, they were flat out lying in your face.

When Donna first saw the gallery she thought it looked a bit out of place on this four block stretch of ritzy shops in downtown Walnut Creek, anchored by names like Neiman Marcus and Saks Fifth Avenue. The strangeness of the place intrigued her, not so much the bland sounding name, enticing her to step into its dark, mysterious confines. *What wild works of imagination were displayed in there? Anything too risqué?* Here was an artsy shop that belonged in Berkeley, Oakland, or San Francisco, certainly not here in lily white suburbia.

So Donna thought, *why not?* And went in, certainly fitting in with the neighborhood, dressed in her pressed and ironed dark gray colored business suit, immaculate as the day she first bought it, with her shiny new pumps. Besides, she was a tad bored. But who could possibly be bored after pocketing twenty thousand dollars?

Donna meandered through the gallery, checking this and that out, walking up to admire that particular bust or to scrutinize a small painting. One thing that struck her as odd was that the place was totally empty! Where was everybody? Not even an employee in sight to greet her. Maybe they were asleep in a back room somewhere. Then she thought about the time of day. Well, it was two o'clock P.M. on a weekday. People still at work. She loved her flexible work schedule that allowed her to go to stores and restaurants when they weren't so crowded. Sometimes she felt like she had the whole joint to herself. That was always nice.

After she rounded a corner in the gallery with its ominous black painted walls, she saw *it.* There *it* was. Waiting for her. A modern style airbrush painting of outer space, specifically focusing on the planet Pluto and beyond. In the upper left hand corner of the portrait, furtively creeping by it seemed, was a metallic spacecraft, hovering above the surface of the planet.

The painting was showcased on a single wall all by itself, enhancing the eerie atmosphere of the piece perfectly. Donna immediately felt at peace when she initially laid her eyes on it, feeling the chilly atmosphere of the universe and finding solace in it from the crazed world she inhabited, overrun by technology, gadgets, and social media. Something about it called out to her. She could relate to it somehow.

Donna had to have it, no matter what the price. And what could be a better way to celebrate the business deal than plunking down some cash for this? *Let's do it.*

From her peripheral vision she saw someone encroaching in on the portrait, a person she hadn't noticed in the gallery before and who must've just come in. A tall man with dark hair and long sideburns, in a vintage 1970s plaid blazer and corduroy pants, appraising the artwork with the utmost discerning eye of the shrewdest art critic. Here was a person who knew their stuff when it came to collecting.

Donna had seen that ravenous eagle eye before in prior business meetings, and not wanting to luck out on obtaining this fantastic gem of a discovery, she propelled herself forward, blocking the painting with her body before the man had a chance to inch his way any closer.

Donna cleared her throat. "I'm sorry, but this painting's already been sold," she lied.

The man looked at her, noticing her for the very first time, probably lost in a dream-like trance, as she had been, by the painting. Only the very best art had that effect on you. She had to admit that, quite frankly, this particular work left her heart racing, perspiring profusely, and feeling lightheaded, almost to the point of fainting. She even had to reach out to the wall to balance herself a couple of times. But it was a good giddiness, she rationalized, not a bad influence.

Does he feel the same thing as me at this moment?

The man shrugged, like it was no biggie, and sauntered off.

Suddenly, from out of nowhere, an African American woman with short black hair done in stylish bangs, approached her with a pleasant grin. For some reason, the woman made Donna think of daytime talk show hosts. She didn't know why that popped in her head, it just did. Maybe it was the shiny gloss and sheen of what the woman applied to her hair. The sudden appearance startled her a little but it was all good.

"If you have any questions about anything, please let me know. My name's Victoria." The woman had a reassuring smile that put her at ease and made her feel at home.

"Uhh, actually I do," Donna replied, nodding at the portrait. "I didn't see a price for that one."

"This one is one of my personal favorites." Victoria stepped closer to it. "For me, it harkens back to the timeless wonder of adventure and exploring the unknown and what lies beyond." Then she flipped through a binder before telling Donna the price.

"I'll take it," Donna responded without hesitation.

"Good choice."

<hr>

"Excuse me, how much are you asking for that?" the tall man with dark hair and long sideburns asked, pointing at an oil painting hanging all by itself in a hidden corner.

Victoria consulted the binder and informed him.

"Who's the artist?"

She looked again. "Hmmm, it doesn't say."

"That's odd." He turned around and admired the framed portrait before him, depicting a stone maze, its walls chiseled to smooth, immaculate perfection, situated on a foggy island in the middle of a large body of water. Standing at the entrance to the maze were two figures in red robes, their faces obscured by hoods.

"Yes. I'm sorry about that." She stood next to him, examining the painting as if she were looking at it for the very first time, but deftly suppressing the fact that she'd seen it hundreds of times already. "What draws you to this particular piece?"

"Well, I'm an anthropology professor, you see, and this artwork speaks both to my academic side because it symbolizes ancient civilization and myth as well as my love for world travel, as represented by the island."

"I see. Which island does it remind you of specifically, Mister..."

"Taylor." He paused for a moment, studying the painting. "The Isle of Man. I led an expedition there years ago." His eyes sparkled a bit at the memory.

She nodded, pursing her lips as she cast a curious eye at him. "Are you biracial?"

Some people would've turned to her and remarked, *'What?'* Or maybe be offended by the question but Taylor just nodded. "Couldn't quite check me off in a box, could you?"

"Nope. You look too much like Keanu Reeves for me to do that."

He grinned. "Aw, that's a nice compliment."

"Are you part Asian, part white?"

"Yes."

"Sorry for probing... just my inquisitive nature I guess. Did you find any interesting artifacts in that place?"

"Indeed. Have many people been inquiring about this painting?" he asked, trying to gauge its popularity.

"Quite a few, actually."

He hated it when salespeople claimed that when it wasn't actually true, simply utilizing that ploy to spike a commission for themselves. However, on the other hand, if it was really generating a lot of buzz, then that was certainly a useful piece of information.

Taylor stepped back and regarded the portrait again for a moment, rubbing his chin in thought. Appraising it once more. "I'd like to buy it." No further questions. Open and shut.

Victoria nodded, flashing him a smile. "Excellent decision, Professor Taylor. You won't be disappointed with your investment. Now if you don't mind waiting for just a moment, I'll draft up your purchase."

❧

Donna mounted the portrait on a pair of hooks on

35

the olive colored wall in her bedroom, right above the dresser bureau. She backpedaled a little, checking to make sure it was centered properly. *Perfecto!* Then she crossed her arms proudly across her chest and marveled at the painting, spellbound.

She stepped closer to it to admire the minute details, the texture of the inks, the perfect symmetry of the spacecraft and realistic rendition of Pluto and the stars. The longer that Donna gazed at it, the more she felt like she was actually there in outer space. *Wow!* Now that was cool.

A moment later, an unexplained headache knotted itself squarely in the middle of her forehead, from out of nowhere, as she was standing there. Throbbing like a power drill gone mad with no signs of quitting. She massaged her brow and took a deep breath. This was followed by an inexplicable bout of intense night chills and sweats and she hugged herself gently, trying to calm herself. She thought that strange considering that all the windows in the room were closed. Where did the draft come from? The icy chill knifed through her flesh and bones like she was submerged in frigid arctic waters.

And if that wasn't enough, Donna suddenly began experiencing an accelerated heartbeat, as if she had just finished running a marathon. She found herself panting like a dog, trying to catch her breath. *Am I coming down with something?* She put her hand to her forehead, trying to gauge if it was unusually warm or not.

Donna took a step back, nearly losing her balance, her knee slamming into the nightstand. "Ouch!" Her right hand caressed her brow again, feeling lightheaded like she was about to faint. She shook her head and body, trying to fight it off, whatever it was that possessed her. She had an important business meeting tomorrow and couldn't afford to be ill. *Seriously.* It meant an opportunity to pocket away more money and she wasn't about to be a no-show for that. *No way.*

Donna maintained her footing and looked up at the

portrait again and, seconds later, found solace and her center by simply staring at it. One look was all it took and there she was, back in the galaxy with the stars. Those awesome stars.

But wait a second... didn't the surface of the painting just move? She could've swore the canvas rose up and down a couple of times, like the human chest expanding in and out when a person was breathing. Maybe she just imagined it. Yeah, that was probably it. She was not going bonkers. At least she hoped she wasn't.

But her heart pumped rapidly like a jackhammer. Like she was racing in that marathon. She mopped the perspiration off her face with some tissue paper. *Why am I sweating so damn much?* Donna was sort of foggy about what occurred next exactly. It certainly was open to interpretation. But from her perspective, and as best as she could describe, something that felt like a magnetic gravitational pull shoved her towards the painting, to the point that she almost lost her balance again and nearly fell headlong to the floor.

After regaining her footing, but before she even had time to react, she was literally swept off her feet by some strong, invisible force and hurled at the portrait. But instead of smashing head on into the canvas she fluidly merged into it, as smooth as liquid, like she was entering a portal into another world. Donna screamed, and continued screaming all the way until she reached the *'other'* side of the painting, where she found herself in a pitch black space.

Only she wasn't standing in a room anymore. She wasn't even sure where she was exactly. It was so dark she couldn't even see her own hand in front of her face. Then she saw them... hundreds, *no* thousands, *no, correction: millions* of stars... her jaw dropped open and she shrieked... they were scattered all around her, *above, below, in front of, behind her,* were these bright stars, those same beautiful stars she was so hypnotized by in the painting. Now it seemed they were in her presence, *literally. Holy cow!* What fluke of nature was *this*? She hadn't the foggiest.

Donna gradually got her bearings and soon realized she was not standing indeed, for she was actually floating! Floating through outer space! Her screams shattered the silent void as she somersaulted her way past stars, spinning round and round, and out of control.

And it was freezing here in space! Wearing nothing but her pajamas. *Oh God, it's icy cold!* Donna looked over her shoulder and saw the planet, Pluto. Her eyes bulged out. *This must be a dream, err, a nightmare...this can't be happening. I'm going to wake up soon and all this will be gone and I'll be back in my apartment like before. Yes, that is what is going to happen. This is 'not' real. This is 'not' real.* Donna kept chanting, "This is not real," to herself over and over again, but when she opened her eyes later, she still saw Pluto and that field of bright stars surrounding her.

Her heart kept pounding as thoughts raced through her head. *What am I going to do? How do I get back home? How did I get 'inside' the painting?* Too many questions and no answers. Donna saw the metallic spacecraft furtively creeping by and tried to grab a hold of it but couldn't hang on. It flew away and she yelled, *"Help!"* But it kept going. Her shouts were futile.

Soon, the freezing temperatures paralyzed her limbs and muscles to the point that she could move no more. Her whole face, body, and brain were numb. She couldn't resist or struggle anymore. Nor could she scream... her mouth and vocal chords ceased to function.

The only sense remaining was her vision and what she saw in front of her moments later made her frown, for she was suddenly puzzled why she couldn't see those beautiful bright stars anymore. *Where'd they all go?* Donna's tragic last thoughts. She continued somersaulting through an infinite ocean of inky darkness, not seeing Pluto, the spacecraft, or anything else. *What happened?*

The last thing that Donna saw before she was sucked into the black hole was simply... pitch blackness. Complete, utter, and eternal pitch blackness.

⹌⹌⹌

Professor Taylor removed the brown butcher paper from the portrait. After securing two hooks on the wall of his study, he mounted the canvas, climbed down the ladder, and took a step back to inspect the job. It was a little crooked so he went up again and repositioned it. He checked it once more and this time it was a thumbs up.

He poured himself a cup of green tea with curls of steam resembling question marks rising from the surface of the water and let it steep before sitting down on an office chair facing the painting. After taking a bite from his Danish pastry, he leaned back and studied the portrait, finding himself gradually mesmerized by it, and *felt* himself at the entrance of that stone maze and felt the cold, misty fog on that island blowing against his face. He could almost wipe the moisture off his cheek and smell the salt water. In that brief moment he was virtually *there*.

Wow, that's intense.

He also realized he had developed a headache. But when he turned away from the painting he no longer felt it, nor did he feel the burning intensity brought on by the hypnosis.

Minutes later, he sipped his tea and returned his gaze to the portrait, sensing the burning obsession again as well as the headache. He averted his eyes, bringing the pastry up to his mouth to take another bite. The glowing desire and headache vanished.

Taylor examined the artwork one more time, feeling the obsession again. This time, it pulled him off the chair, pushing him towards the painting, his feet moving on their own. *Something* was forcing him to go in that direction. But who or what he didn't know. It was weird, but certainly no stranger than some of the other things he encountered before in his profession as well as his dealings with the paranormal.

All he knew was that he felt *different* and not himself when he was paying attention to the painting. He recalled feeling the same way when he was looking at it back in the gallery but dismissed it at the time, figuring it was due to job stress.

Hmmm. He put down his cup and cautiously approached the portrait, deliberately keeping his head low and not looking at it. He decided to conduct an experiment to test a theory of his. As soon as he was one foot away from the portrait, he raised his head and stared up at it. Those obsessive feelings returned in an instant, dragging him to the portrait, and slamming him into it. *Jeez, this portrait is ravenous!* It rattled against the wall, like something demoniacally possessed. Taylor felt the painting trying to suck him into the canvas but he looked away in the nick of time and pushed himself away from it with all his strength, backpedaling until his knees collided with a low table, sending him crashing to the ground.

He got back up. *Now would be a good time to get a refund for this thing before the warranty expires*, he joked to himself. Taylor glanced down at the day's newspaper lying on his desk, with the bold, black headline of an article catching his eye.

It read: **Walnut Creek Man Disappears Shortly After Purchasing Painting**

He picked up the newspaper and scanned the article, his brow furrowing as he processed the details. *Bought at the same place, the Olson Galleria. Huh! Small world.* He scratched the back of his head. *The man's brother said he went to his house and didn't find him there. After checking with other family members as well as friends and coworkers, the police were notified and followed up, not finding Hal Perez anywhere...no trace of his body, no blood, no note, no social media post, nothing. 'He vanished mysteriously without a single trace,' Perez's brother remarked.*

Taylor dropped the newspaper back on the desk, went to his laptop and opened it up to conduct a quick search about this gallery to see if there had been any other unusual incidents associated with it. Nothing popped up.

It was time to do a little snooping around.

⟶⟩⟨⟩⟨

As he was walking on the treadmill at the campus gym, Taylor scrolled down a page on his phone, reading a small news blurb at the bottom. Another missing person, this time a young businesswoman named Donna Andrews, who also happened to buy a piece of art from the Olson Galleria. Now how odd was that? Coincidence? Maybe, maybe not. Perhaps it was just a popular place to get art. Anyway, shortly after purchasing a painting there, Miss Andrews also disappeared without a trace it seemed. When she failed to respond to numerous inquiries from her next door neighbor, the neighbor grew worried and concerned, saying it was very uncharacteristic of her not to reply. The neighbor claimed Miss Andrews always promptly got back to him whenever he called or texted her. So this was unusual.

Taylor took his eyes off the phone for a moment to increase the elevation settings on the treadmill before scrolling further down the page to continue reading. He really needed to push himself on this workout to shed all the damage those Danish pastries did to his body. Enough said. Back to the article at hand. The neighbor informed the police about Miss Andrews not being in her apartment, stirring a bit of a panic within the complex. Was she kidnapped? Sexually assaulted, etc.? Perhaps abducted by one of those 'sneaky foreign businessmen,' as one of her other neighbors labeled them, which she constantly interacted with. 'You simply can't trust those kinds of folks,' the neighbor chimed in with his two cents.

Taylor shook his head. *Ignorance and prejudice is what is going to bring down this nation.* He kept reading. The police questioned Miss Andrews' family, relatives, friends, and known business associates but none of them could shed any light on where she could possibly be.

"It all started with that dog-gone painting," her

friend was quoted as saying. "She became obsessed with it and never stopped raving about it. She referred to it like it was a person."

Taylor turned away from his phone. *Exactly how I felt, too, when I stared at my portrait for prolonged periods of time.* Something about those paintings...as if they possessed a living soul of their own. *As if they were alive.* The power and energy inside of them... did they thrive off of killing human beings or harming them? What drove them to do what they almost *did* to him? Not to mention the others. And most importantly, what happened to those missing people?

Were they still alive? His optimistic ego wanted to believe that.

※

Victoria looked at Taylor. "It's weird but I felt the exact symptoms as you did... the rapid heartbeat, everything. How eerie." She shook her head.

"That's not the only word I'd used to describe it. What else can you tell me about Mr. Perez and Miss Andrews?"

She looked at his business card, pursing her lips together hesitantly. "Paranormal investigator, huh?"

He nodded, wondering if he alarmed her or had freaked her out more than he had anticipated. Most people were curious, if anything, when he told them.

"Are you working with the police? Because I've already told them everything..." A little hint of annoyance in her voice now. Just a *tad*.

"No, I'm not. Just a good Samaritan who likes to stick his nose into unusual things and help out if I can."

Victoria cocked one eye at him. "Are you one of those folks who think that most people are generally good?"

"Are you going to be a hater if I am?"

She chuckled, shaking her head. "You're too much..." She glanced at his card again. "Professor Taylor. I gotta hand it to you, though. I like you but you're a little strange. But strange can be good."

"I'll take that as a compliment."

Victoria leaned back in her office chair. "Why do you care about these folks who you don't even know? Let alone never met."

"Might as well ask me why do I care about a huge lecture hall packed full of young college freshmen who I don't know from Adam."

She regarded him for a moment. "Do tell."

"Because they deserve a chance, not just to succeed in life, but to be heard. Just like these two customers of yours. They're people who matter to someone."

She seemed satisfied with that answer, nodding, and paused for a moment. "Aside from them coming in and buying the artwork I didn't know anything else about them, I'm afraid."

He crossed his legs. "Nothing weird stuck out in your head?"

"No."

"Where did you get the paintings from?"

"You know, that's the interesting thing. They were already here when I started my employment. Nobody knew where they originated from." Victoria shrugged. "Maybe they came with the gallery."

"Who was the previous shopkeeper?"

She pursed her lips again. "An old man from Europe. Nice guy. He gave me this job, for which I'm eternally grateful." She shook her head, staring ahead as she reflected back. "I was struggling to find work at the time, having a difficult period landing interviews. I sent out tons of resumes but got no calls. Finally, this gig came along, and right in the nick of time cuz my rent was already three weeks overdue that month...so this job was definitely a Godsend, a blessing, and I'll always be appreciative towards that old man. I think of him from time to time."

Taylor had his pen poised over his notepad. "What's his name and do you have his contact information?"

"He's dead."

"Somehow I knew you were going to say that. Any

clue where he acquired the portraits from?"

Victoria shook her head. "He never revealed that."

"Was that because he was harboring a secret you think or you never asked?"

"Both."

"You know, all the portraits seem like they were created by the same hand. Do you know who the artist is?"

"Unfortunately, that's a mystery as well."

"Marvelous." His mind jumped on to the next idea. "Perhaps this old man has family members, friends, or business associates who know about these paintings."

Victoria shot him a look. "And you want my help, I assume, in tracking them down?"

"Well, I was hoping you had an inkling that was the case."

※

Google kept spitting out, *'Did not find any matches based on your search,'* after Taylor typed in a bunch of different phrases and key words in succession.

"Shoot!" he muttered.

Victoria pulled her chair a little closer to him, looking at the screen of his laptop. The café they were in was just a couple of blocks away from the gallery, one of those new age kind of places that were currently all the rage here in Walnut Creek, with lots of Buddhist imagery and relaxing new age music piping through tiny speakers. Today it was something with a lot of soft, techno drumbeats and chanting. There were small statues and busts of Buddha strategically placed at various spots in the café (practicing good Feng Shui here), as well as related artwork hanging on the walls and even a miniature water fountain at the entrance to greet customers with its soothing sounds.

He found the gentle trickling sound of water flowing was having an effect on him, for it was incredibly calming. He felt like meditating.

"Punch in mysterious old men in the European art world, 2016," she suggested.

"Are you serious?"

"*Deadly.*"

"Your wish is my command." And he typed it in.

A plethora of articles popped up. Taylor tilted the computer towards her so she could see better.

"Any of these names look familiar?" he asked.

She studied the list of items, shaking her head with a frown.

He clicked the mouse, going to the next few pages but she didn't recognize anything.

Victoria leaned back in her chair, brushing her stylish bangs away from her eyes, her brow knotted in concentration. "God, what was his name?" She sighed, shutting her eyes. "Sssss... Ss... Sa... Sasha?" She shook her head. "Sss... Ste... Ste... Stefan? No." Victoria pondered things further, snapping her fingers a moment later. "Victor! That's it!"

"Remember his last name?"

Her forehead creased in wrinkles once more. "Afraid not. Sorry."

"Don't be. This is still helpful." His fingers tapped the keyboard, adding *'mysterious old men in the European art world, 2016,'* after the name she supplied.

Seconds passed before a fresh cropping of links populated the screen.

"This looks promising," he remarked, clicking on an article, zapping them to a page with a color photograph of a man with iron gray hair and a matching bushy mustache and beard. The caption under the photo read: ***Victor Schroeder, circa 2014***

"That him?"

Her eyes lit up in recognition. "Yes. Probably taken right before he passed away."

Taylor scanned the article. "Resided in the Bay Area before moving back to his native Germany where he eventually died... owned and operated an art gallery, bringing many paintings with him from Europe, show-casing them there... had various gala receptions at said gallery, with many of the artists in attendance. Ah, we're getting warm." He returned his attention to the article, frowning. "Doesn't say who... hmm. Dead end." The gentle sound of the water flowing at the water fountain centered him and made him feel more relaxed. "Is there anything back at the gallery that could help narrow down our search?"

"Just the paintings themselves," she replied.

"Back to the genesis. Do the other paintings impact you the same way and give you the same symptoms?"

She nodded. "I've learned not to look at any of them for too long."

"And yet it wasn't until now that they've been suspected of causing these freakish incidents. Why now all of a sudden?"

Victoria shrugged. "Beats me."

They collected all the portraits in the gallery, including the ones sold to Hal Perez and Donna Andrews, and piled them on top of one another in a back room. When he had explained to Perez's and Andrews' next of kin the reasoning behind their request of wanting the items back, they displayed no reluctance in releasing the artwork to them.

"Don't stare at the paintings!" Taylor warned, tossing Perez's medieval portrait onto the mounting heap.

Victoria stood back as he uncapped a small tank of gasoline, splashing the liquid on the assortment of paintings, before taking out a matchbook. After lighting a single stick he hurled it on top of the pile and it went ablaze immediately.

They both retreated far away from the growing orange flames, covering their noses and mouths from the toxic fumes, turning around to gaze at the small conflagration.

For a moment, Taylor thought he heard human screams and shrieks emanating from those portraits as they were being incinerated but he wasn't absolutely certain. Maybe it was just all in his head.

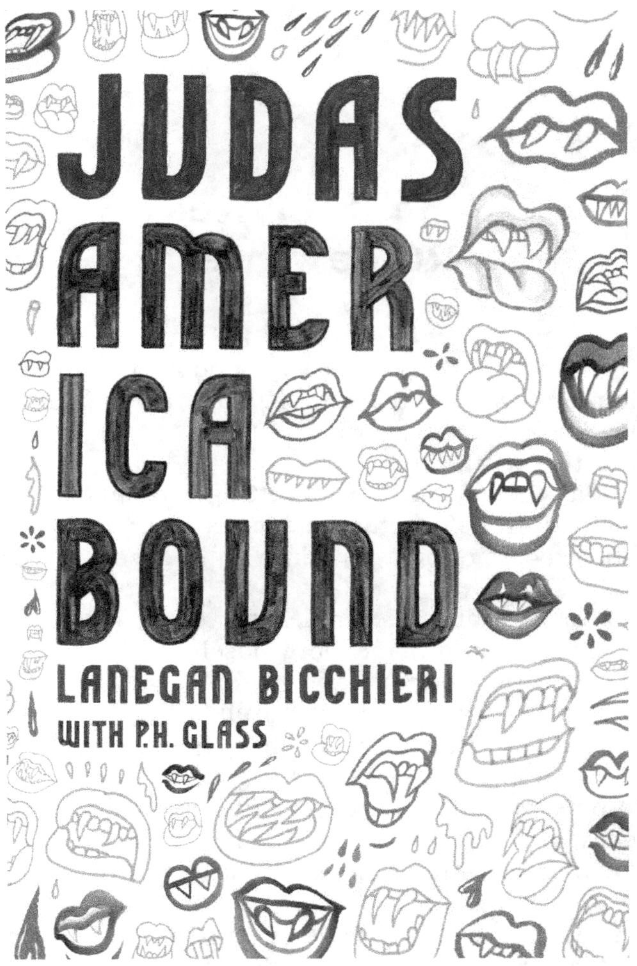

Judas Sycamore is a very nontraditional man. He's a smoker. He's introverted. He loves men more than women though he does enjoy them... and he hunts vampires.

Journeying home in the early 1910s, he's on his way to hunt down a vampire lord, one who robbed him of an old flame, but things become a bit complicated for everyone involved.

Available at www.irbstore.co
Or use the order form at the back of this book!

The Uninvited
RC deWinter

When I got up today I opened every window in the house.
Room to room I yanked those sashes up;
every day I do it with more violence.
No matter the weather I have to,
for every day the oily perfume of rotting fish hangs,
a heavy cloud, transforming the simple,
automatic process of breathing into an undesirable necessity.

I have company that refuses to leave,
refuses to speak, follows me more closely
than a shadow on a sunny day.
Wherever I am there it is—a silent hulk
squatting in the middle of the kitchen, the parlor, the study.
If I take a shower it squeezes its unwelcome bulk
right in there with me—no soap scrubs away that stench—
and every night it sits, never blinking, watching me
as I fall exhausted into never restful sleep.

It's a twisted version of the fabled elephant in the room.
Not that I'm afraid to address it—it's obvious I'll never get an
answer.
I am no sinner pursued by a relentless loving God.
This is a cipher silently mocking my ignorance,
leaving me trapped in the hell of no forgiveness
for a sin I did not commit.

Lovecraft's Paranormal Fiction
Daniel R. Robichaud

While H. P. Lovecraft's reputation stands based on the two best known cycles of fiction he wrote throughout his career—the Cthulhu Mythos tales and his Dreamland fantasies—he also had more than his share of standalones and one-offs. Some of these fall more easily into a realm of storytelling best described as paranormal fiction.

These tales involve more-or-less normal folks interacting with the otherworldly, a localized bizarre-ness, the unexpected comes about on a more personal scale instead of the level of monstrous mythologies or Lord Dunsany-inspired fantasies. However, even in these unassociated tales readers will find many of the themes that motivated those better-known works. This article will delve into a few of these other stories in order to piece together the author's approach to paranormal topics.

The Past Looms Large

Lovecraft's Cthulhu Mythos stories posit humanity as an insignificant presence in the cosmos. Greater, grander entities and designs populate the infinite universe than the residents of our little planet. In the author's paranormal tales, humanity retains its smallness. However, the looming forces that drive stories in this vein are not titans, either cosmic entities or their servitors. Instead, our own history is the specter that looms across the aeons, pushing and pulling human beings along courses toward inescapable horror.

Take, for example, the story "The Tomb". It first appeared in the March, 1922, issue of The Vagrant. The story tackles the obsessions its protagonist, Jervas Dudley, has for the titular location near his childhood home—a mausoleum belonging to the Hyde mansion, which burned down many years before.

The fascination begins with Jervis's childhood discovery of a locked mausoleum entrance. A curious child, he is nevertheless unable to gain entry. Showing patience few children ever can, Jervas waits several years, his enthrallment growing, and even sleeps outside the door. Eventually, he becomes convinced that someone dwells within the mausoleum after seeing a light winking out. Discovering a key secreted away in a rotten chest, he makes his way inside the tomb and discovers a coffin with his own name upon it. Instead of sleeping in the grass outside the place, he takes to sleeping within the building and the coffin itself. By the end of the tale, he is convinced he has experienced an encounter with paranormal forces, which both showed him the last night of destruction for the Hyde mansion and whispered assurances of his place in the tomb. Jervas soon believes himself to be the reincarnation of Jervas Hyde. The end of the tale veers into questions of mental stability or reincarnation: Is Jervas mad or is he in fact touched by the otherworldly?

"The Tomb" is a brief tale, but in its short page count we witness several of the elements that haunt the author's non-mythic cycle stories. The Hyde mansion, ruined as it is, was a site of debauchery and decadence in the past. The ramifications of those qualities have survived the house and family that did not, and they plague the living decades of years later. Jervas Dudley is a man susceptible to the influence of the grave, and while one can read the story as a descent into obsession, it reads equally well as the character being touched by weird, ghostly forces.

Some might point to this theme as one more instance of the oft-cited "Inherited Guilt" idea, wherein crimes committed by a family's forbears return to haunt their descendants. That idea maps more easily to a story like "The Rats in the Walls," where a man returns to his ancestral home and learns about horrible secrets locked underneath the property. However, Inherited Guilt is at best a limited variation to the theme proposed here. Jervas is not necessarily the literal descendant of that lost, decadent Hyde family. Therefore, he cannot possess Inherited Guilt. In fact, it might be a titanic force of another sort at work here, blindly searching out a likely victim.

What is the nature of the forces afflicting "The Tomb's" protagonist? Are the dreams and whispers actual spirits or are they instead the manifestations of some greater power, against which Jervas is ill equipped to triumph. I argue that "The Tomb" show-cases a situation in which history itself has come to haunt the living. Its manipulation and motivations are as unstoppable as any titanic entity. Perhaps it is even more powerful than the author's own Great Old Ones since it has no physical shape and is instead the most fiendish specter or incorporeal presence the author ever manifested. Jervas was a malleable, sensitive consciousness this manipulator bent to its whims.

Our Future is Someone Else's Past

In fact, Lovecraft's paranormal fiction all relies on history to some degree or another. In this context, history cannot be viewed only as events recorded in a book. Often, we conceive of history as a series of past events that culminate in the present, however in Lovecraft's works and particularly in his paranormal fiction, history is a continuum, a line stretching from the dawn of the universe to its end. The characters in his plots are caught at various points on this line. His protagonists often look backwards along this line to their own ancestral pasts. Narratives such as Lovecraft's short novel The Case of Charles Dexter Ward is a great example of this, positing a witch who died in colonial days returning to life in the modern era and plaguing his descendant. However, this does not need to be the case in all circumstances. In several circumstances, the otherworldly influence can just as easily come from further up the timeline than the protagonist, passing into the character's life from some remote future on its way to a terrible past.

The novella The Shadow Out of Time demonstrates how Lovecraft's strange beings can move their consciousness across space and time. In this story, they subvert protagonist Nathaniel Wingate Peaslee's conscious control of his own body. Although the being's influence has the signs of a spiritual possession, Peaslee is enduring an assault from an alien consciousness. These mind swaps started as a means of exploring history through a kind of boots-on-the-ground or fly-on-the-wall mode, an observational archaeology if you will; however, the strange process then became a means for that race to escape destruction by taking over consciousness of cone-shaped beings in Earth's prehistory. When that race is destroyed, the presences will then occupy beings that follow long after humanity's passing.

The Shadow Out of Time can be considered a part of the more cosmic-oriented Cthulhu Mythos cycle of tales. However, it also falls into the standalone pieces, as well. Less concerned with the machinations of titans, gods, and their servants, the novella instead postulates a lone protagonist grappling with memories of a future and past that are not his own. Appearing at the end of Lovecraft's career—only one more story Lovecraft finished himself would appear before his death—The Shadow Out of Time highlights this idea of history extending in both directions. According to studies of consciousness in animals, the concept of dividing time into past, present, and future is more of a manmade concept. As with all of mankind's creations, it is flawed in its design and potentially incongruous with the way the universe actually works. Beings capable of moving through time can move human beings much the same way that the past rose from its unquiet grave to influence the present as in stories like "The Tomb".

Memories and the Consciousness Are the Real Haunts

A haunt is a word with multiple meanings. On the

one hand, it is a place visited and revisited over time. On the other hand, haunt is also a word associated with ectoplasmic or incorporeal beings, the residue of humans who have died. On the final hand, it is an active word associated with what ghosts do in their houses.

Lovecraft's paranormal pieces play with all definitions of the word, applying them to memory and consciousness. These three interpretations form the fundamental means by which the human mind interacts with the past, the present, and conceives of the future. In Lovecraft's works, memory and consciousness are also battlegrounds of sorts, a haunt (metaphoric location) where paranormal forces (actual haunters) influence and drive (haunt, in its active sense) human beings. The results are never beneficial to the subject.

Take, for example, "Beyond the Wall of Sleep," which predates the aforementioned The Shadow Out of Time by almost two decades. In this piece, an Appalachian man, Joe Slater, is being held for murder. He suffers nightly visitations from an otherworldly being with unknown motivations. When an intern at the asylum repurposes a telepathy machine to speak to Slater's mind during one of these visitations, he comes to learn that an otherworldly presence is possessing the man, driving away Slater's consciousness. The intern learns that this being is a bodiless entity engaged in a struggle against a similar being out in the vastness of space. As with time, distance has little meaning to the cosmic entities, they are entangled with themselves and each other in a similar way quarks are, influencing one another across impossible distances through a kind of "spooky physics." Like the creatures in The Shadow Out of Time, the being possessing Slater is capable of pushing its consciousness into another's physical body. The tale ends with Slater's death as well as the birth of a brilliant star in the heavens—a symbol of the strange being's conflict with its nemesis. Joe Slater's consciousness is a haunt, which is haunted in turn by an otherworldly haunter.

Next consider, "The Outsider," a tale in which a first person narrator emerges from a world of catacombs, the only world he has known, to find himself in the presence of a debauched party. The story is driven by faulty memory, and the finale of the piece finds the unnamed narrator on the receiving end of a revelation that reshapes his consciousness, as it were, by fundamentally altering his awareness of himself.

The above present two examples of many. Memory and consciousness are key concepts found throughout Lovecraft's fiction, including both the standalone tales as well as his more infamous story cycles. These two concepts drive much of the horror in his fiction. Memory and consciousness are both the most often assailed aspects of his protagonists; after all, insanity represses memory as well as one's awareness of oneself. How many dreams are invaded, how many bodies are claimed by consciousness that are not their own, how many stories include some past evil rising like a tsunami to wash aside a present day protagonist's sense of himself, and how many memories are scrambled by association with the ineffable? Death of the body might end several of the author's stories, but its sting is less horrifying than the destruction of the narrator's self. In fact, death of the flesh is seldom without a preceding death of the "mind" or con-sciousness. One could easily speculate that this may stem from Lovecraft's own biography—his parents both died in asylums—but such a reading is spurious at best. Instead, we can appreciate the phenomenon on its own merits, as a source of Otherness that can reside within even the most stable minds and bodies.

Concluding Remarks

Lovecraft's standalone fiction will never find equal popular or critical footing with those in his story cycles. However, though they might be minor entries in his oeuvre, the tales are nevertheless intriguing explorations of otherworldly influences over normal people. Grappling with history, the future, memory, and consciousness, these stories present the chilling results when a paranormal world intersects with the everyday. Although he has little sympathy for superstition, even in his weird tales, Lovecraft has never shied away from the otherworldly. Though the stories themselves are unconnected, the obsessive, mechanistic mind behind them was the same. An appreciation of the themes running through Lovecraft's "lesser" stories lends itself to a deeper appreciation of the craft operating behind all of his prose.

The past, the present, and the future are essentially human concepts, the source of many trials and travails, as well as a part of our drives to excel. To whit: if we practice now, we will improve in the future. However, in the Lovecraft Worlds, this is not the case at all. Time is a boogeyman all its own, either serving as a concourse from which threats can manifest or a threat all its own. These threats endanger the mind, the consciousness.

There in a nutshell is the core conceit powering Lovecraft's fiction and cosmic horror in general. The universe may be infinite, its horrors either timeless or standing outside of time, and the human mind's coping mechanisms with the world and universe it occupies are fragile. Consciousness is vital to the sense of self, and yet consciousness is not a suit of hardened armor. It is as frail as tissue paper, easily torn by passing supernatural or paranormal elements.

Unavoidable
Tyree Campbell

His name was John-Wadi Karwani, he was twenty-five years old, and he had a mixed lineage. A Palestinian Jew—Wadi meant "river" in Arabic—he had grown up in Anathoth, in what was before the war the West Bank, and he was in fact a citizen of the Hashemite Kingdom of Jordan. Because he was a Jew, he also possessed Israeli papers, and long after the war, it was these papers that enabled him to, among other things, hike in the mountains north of the Dead Sea.

Hiking had been a hobby of his—perhaps more accurately a compulsive pastime—for the past ten years, after he had grown tired of hearing from his father that Anathoth was the birthplace of Jeremiah and therefore a certain greatness was expected of him. Indifferent at school—he held a degree in geology from the University of Tel Aviv, where he had done barely enough to prevent his father from admonishing him— he made a modest living by assisting and advising American archaeologists at various digs. He had some skill at sifting, and on several occasions had noticed teeth and fragments of pottery that others had missed. But on this day he was hiking, wandering, because his father, over the tears and objections of his mother, had exiled him from the house.

She was, he thought, nudging a cactus with his boot toe, her own Wailing Wall. John-Wadi himself had little interest in the traumas of the past. Yes, digs were a fine place to meet young women who occasionally were interestingly clad, but they were too focused on the ground to look up to him.

Now he had gone out into the desert mountains, as so many prophets had before him, but he was not looking for inspiration. He simply had to get away.

Eight kilometers and four hours and two canteens brought him to Ramah, hardly a metropolis, but larger than Anathoth. There he replenished his water supply, sat at an outdoor café in the shade, and wondered what to do next.

The girl who sauntered by gave him a notion, and she even glanced at him as she passed. College student, he decided; she looked to be about that age. Contemporary attire: a simple, pale blue jersey and blue jean cutoffs revealed skin that had spent many hours outdoors. He speculated, and considered, and finally concluded that she might be a digger at some obscure site nearby. He straightened his cap to peer at her as she walked into the sun. It was tempting to follow her, not only for diversion, but perhaps for that one job, that one task, that might make all the difference in his life.

He watched her walk away, buttocks pumping like pistons to propel her forward. She had a good stride, as if she knew where she was going and the best way to get there. Unlike me, he thought, as he addressed a cup of black coffee. I'm just going, and I'll get there when I stop. He cast a final glance toward the girl, only to discover that she had disappeared.

As the wall on this side of the street was a façade of quarried stone from Jordanian days, there was nowhere for her to have gone, unless she had reached the corner of the street in the time it had taken him to drink a sip of hot coffee. She hadn't run, though a part of him wished she had. Barring an empirical determination, he was as certain as could be that she wore nothing under the jersey.

Karwani sighed. Still... of the young women he had met at digs, only two had taken any after-dig interest in him, and that fleetingly. He returned, somewhat sadder, to his coffee.

The sun passed behind the façade and brought an additional measure of shade to the white umbrella under which he was sitting. There was still time to wander, and the street led out of the town and into the hills. He dreamed of finding a hitherto-unnoticed site somewhere and of raking in a bit of the fame and remuneration that often accompanied such discoveries.

Certainly the Middle East was replete with them. Doubtless thousands had been all but destroyed in the incessant warfare over the millennia, but still...

He sighed again, and drained the cup.

On the other side of the street, one of the shops rented bicycles. Karwani selected one with a basket for his backpack, and with sturdy off-road tires, and paid for overnight. He had a choice: north to Mizpah or east to Geba. The two towns were roughly equidistant from Ramah. To the east, ancient beds delineated water flows into the Jordan. They swayed him. He climbed on and began to pedal.

Already with a sheen of perspiration on his olive-tan, soon he was drenched. The Arabs with their bulky clothing had the answer to desert survival, and for a few years during his childhood Karwani had opted now and then for similar clothing. Not lately, however. It was difficult to be attractive when bundled up, and besides, riding a bicycle required freedom of movement.

The street joined a dirt road that took him in an easterly direction and out into what he thought of as badlands. Here was the land of lizards and snakes and scorpions, although none were likely to be found out in the open, for the sun would quickly kill them. To the southeast he could see sprawling Geba. The road eventually would take him there—he had traveled it before—and he might arrange a place to stay for the night.

He had just entered an ancient riverbed when the front tire of his bicycle began to lose air. Perhaps had it been the rear tire, he might have pressed onward, but it was the front tire that took the brunt of resistance from the sand. Although he was in good riding conditions, his legs were not up to five more miles of that. Accordingly, he dismounted, kicked at the offending tire with his boot, and spoke as if he were about to violate a couple of the Commandments.

If the bicycle gave a response, it was inaudible save the final hissing of the air from the tire.

A nearby large stone with a relatively flat top offered Karwani a perch, and he sat down to take stock. He had two canteens of water, more than enough to allow him to return on foot to Ramah or to push on to Geba. But in this desolate land there was no shade. He wondered how Jeremiah had survived. But the prophet undoubtedly had been wearing desert garb, and knew where the oases were, and wouldn't decline a lizard or two. In frustration Karwani threw up his hands and slapped them down on his knees. The dry air absorbed the sound.

He was alone.

Shelter. He had to find shade if he remained here in the desert. With no oases in evidence, he looked all around for a cave, or even a crevasse. The sun was still a good four hours from the horizon. It would do him no good to remain out in it, but he was not looking forward to spending the night in a darkness lit only by stars. The sun could be deadly, but so could the nocturnal denizens.

Karwani was unable to make a decision. He might as well have been catatonic. He was sitting, sat, continued to sit. Nothing came to mind. Only bits of grit moved, carried by mild gusts of wind heading from the uplands and down toward the river. The wind whispered as it passed over and around him, tousling his dark brown hair. Or was it a voice...

Karwani growled at himself. *Already I'm hallucinating.*

He remembered kicking at a cactus on his way to Ramah. Cacti held water. He was not prepared to chew cactus pulp, however, not until he had exhausted the canteens. Still, he did not have to die from thirst.

The wind continued to sough. Perhaps, he thought, the words were in Aramaic. An ancient wind, bearing messages he had no chance of deciphering.

Finally he said, to himself, "Do something."

Okay. What?

He reasoned it out. If he was going to find a cave, it would be in the river's bank, not on the flat of the bed. Even if there were no caves, the irregular wall of that bank might provide some respite from the sun. He stood up, retrieved his backpack and his canteens and, abandoning the bicycle, headed down the channel. About fifty meters ahead there was a bend toward the north where he might find shade from the sun now at his back and to the west.

The wind continued to communicate with him. It even seemed to be weeping, as if to provide him with fresh water. He *was* hallucinating. But the sand and detritus in the ancient riverbed was real enough, and from time to time he stumbled on the irregular surface. Sweat dribbled from under the cap and into his eyes, the salt stinging him and blurring his vision. The land became one great smear of browns and tans and yellows, interrupted here and there by tiny bits of color—smooth, water-washed stones from somewhere else. As he rounded the curve of the riverbed, heat shimmered the air. And in the bank to his left...

Was that a hole? It certainly looked dark enough. At one time, geologically, it might have been a narrow crevasse, but the ravages of time and the occasional tremor had broken loose the rock that formed the mouth of the crevasse, and had blocked most of the entrance. There was only a hole about two meters off the ground, and just large enough, perhaps, for him to crawl through. If he wanted to...

Behind him, gravel crunched. Even as he spun around, she said, "What did you find?"

Fate meant nothing to Karwani, who had yet to control his own, but he did hold that what would be, would be. The girl from the sidewalk, like himself, had evidently set out for Geba along this very same riverbed. The bicycle she rode was tagged with the same business logo as his own. She came to a stop and slid forward from seat to plant both feet firmly in the sand.

"A cave?" she asked.

Belatedly Karwani realized that she was riding a man's bicycle. In fact...it looked like his. Had she repaired it? If so, how? And how had she gotten out here to it?

"I don't know," he replied. The presence of her

negated the need for questions and doubts. "I was going to climb up there and look." He removed a torchlight from his backpack. "I just hope I don't meet one of the crawlies," he said, as he began to climb up over the fallen rocks.

"You won't, not in there," said the girl. "And I'm coming, too."

"All right," he said reluctantly. "But be careful."

Reaching the top of the debris, and with an eye for anything that moved, he shined the light into the cave and slowly poked his head and shoulders into the opening. The interior was deeper than he thought. The light dissipated among shadows, and he was unable to see a rear wall to the chamber. An unfamiliar smell reached him—hot, musty, with just a hint of decomposition. Something had died in there. Died long ago.

The girl nudged him, a shove against his butt. He recoiled, pulled back, and glared down at her.

"Let me see," she said, before he could protest.

Incongruously, he tried a flirt. "I don't know," he said. "It's awfully intimate in there, and I don't even know your name."

She grinned. "I don't know yours."

He told her. In return she gave him Rachel. He waited for the rest. "Just Rachel," she insisted.

Karwani sighed. Another stillborn relationship. He ducked his head back into the opening and began to worm his way in. The rockfall below had a gentler slope to it, easier to descend, except that he was going head-first. Old cobwebs with desiccated husks clung to his hands and arms and clothing as he got himself into a position where he could reverse his body. Unable to control the torchlight because he needed both hands, he tossed it down onto a patch of sand, where it illuminated the ceiling. He was feeling his way down when Rachel blocked the light from outside.

"Can you see anything?" she called.

"I'm a little busy at the moment."

Karwani reached with his feet, touched sand, and managed to stand up. Despite the heat outside, the temperature here was cool and dry, and his sweaty skin began to chill him. He retrieved the torch, and turned around to shine it for the girl, only to find her standing before him. Startled, he backed away a step, stumbled, and would have fallen had she not steadied him. Light swung, briefly casting his shadow on the wall.

After she released him, he trailed the light along first one wall and then the other as they penetrated deeper into the cave. Hope welled within him, for this might be a *find* after all. He might even gain a name for himself, if something significant turned up. So far, the sand and ceiling and walls were devoid of signs of occupancy, but sifting for shards and other artifacts might prove useful.

"You're awfully quiet," said Rachel.

"I don't know whether to be excited..."

She touched his shoulder, and pointed. An opening to the left might prove more promising. They took it, and almost immediately found themselves inside a chamber. Jaw dropped, he staggered forward, shining the light this way and that, little sounds of amazement practically drooling from his lips.

"Are you seeing this?" he asked.

She did not answer.

He passed the light more slowly around the chamber. Each of the three walls had been drilled somehow, so that they were perforated with pigeon-holes. Each of them appeared to be of a size that allowed a fist easily to pass. Perhaps half of the holds contained what looked like the wooden handle to a scroll.

"What *is* this place?" he murmured.

The response was a susurration of air: Zelzah. The word, if word it was, meant little to him. Someone was buried here, that was all he could recall.

Presently awe brought him to a state of paralysis. Despite his experience at other digs, he did not know what to do. Silence reigned... but not quite. There was his own rapid and shallow breathing, but there was... something else.

Someone was... crying?

He broke free from himself and turned around. The girl was gone.

Story of my life.

"Rachel?"

The name echoed throughout the cave.

Torn between her and the possibility of scrolls, Karwani cast his die. Girls were ubiquitous, and eventually he would meet one. Caves with scrolls, on the other hand...

Shining the torch, cautiously he reached for a handle, in a slot at eye level. With utmost delicacy he tugged on it. The end of the scroll was now visible. It looked like parchment. It appeared to be relatively new. He'd seen one of the Qumram scrolls, how it flaked apart, with each tiny flake bearing the fragment of a letter. He'd watched while it was evaluated. The letter might be a *gimel* or a *khahf* or any one of twenty others. It was painstaking work. Lifetimes had been devoted to it. While he had no desire to spend his life in such a tedious activity, he did try to be careful with the parchment as he slowly tugged the scroll free. In the light from the torch, he now had no doubt that the parchment was of recent production.

That made no sense.

The light continued to illuminate the interior of the slot. There was something else inside it. Squinting, he peered at it. A small container of some kind, conical, with a conical lid. What archaeologists called biconical. Often enough, they proved to be...

Karwani swallowed the hard lump that had just formed in his throat.

...proved to be... urns.

Somewhere else in the cave, the weeping continued.

Everything makes sense, his father had told him, *if you study long enough.*

Karwani heaved a sardonic laugh. "Even this?"

He tried another handle, removing the scroll just far enough to identify it as such. Behind it he could make out another biconical shape. His lips and throat were dry. He tried a few sips from the canteen. It did not help much.

A light breeze made the hair on the back of his neck rustle against his collar. He whirled around, the beam from the torch darting, searching. There was nothing there.

He tried again. "Rachel!"

Echoes laughed at him. His breathing caught and held momentarily, then released. The enormity of where he was and how he had come to be there began to sink in. Scrolls and urns on the one side, a very strange girl on the other. Where was the balance?

He stepped from the chamber and encountered a light gray mist. Heat had evaporated water trapped in the sand. He'd seen this before, on a dig in the Negev. Far ahead, the opening to the cave beckoned him. He'd seen enough. All he had to do now was report it—and hope someone believed him, so that he might gain credit for the find.

Sand shifted—a gust of air. The torchlight put a shadow puppet of the movement on the wall. Karwani's heart stuttered, just once. Even the Dead Sea caves held ghosts. This one...

"Rachel, where are you?"

"Here."

He whirled, seeking the source of the voice. The cave was empty. Perhaps she was in the chamber... but how could she have gotten there? He was standing near the opening. Was there another chamber? Slowly he made his way over the sand further into the cave.

"Rachel?"

"In here." Her voice sounded tight, as if she had been crying.

The torchlight revealed several more openings. The sound of her voice seemed to come from all of them. He glanced over his shoulder, and turned around. The opening to the cave seemed far away. The urge to flee shook him. He was underground. Previous digs had already been exposed, and he worked in sunlight. Girls did not just disappear. Rachel did not sound as if she was in any danger. But if she was, how could he leave her?

No, he had to find her. He had to at least do that much. If you study long enough, everything makes sense.

"In here," she whispered.

The next opening on the left. Karwani was certain of it. Air flowed around him, turning the mist into wisps. Had she found another entrance? He crept to the opening and cautiously peered around the corner, shining the torch. The chamber was empty, but the walls were lined with more pigeonholes, many with handles protruding. He stepped into the chamber. How many of these scrolls, how many urns?

Directly behind him, she said, "Hundreds."

Karwani made a valiant but unsuccessful effort to leap out of his own skin. He turned, stumbled, and fell back onto the sand. No one was there. A clump of mist drifted, nothing more.

The hair on his arms began to stand. The back of his neck itched. Something was not right. Half a minute later, still sitting on the sand, his mind caught up with his vision. His heart felt hollow, drained of blood.

The mist was drifting *against* the air flow.

Coalescing...

He could see through it.

And then he could not.

The apparition that had taken shape from the mist was that of a dark-haired woman of his mother's age, dressed in white robes that covered her from neck to feet.

To feet that hovered about ten centimeters above the sand.

Her facial structure was similar to Rachel's. It was as if the girl had aged thirty years and died, and was here now.

Eyes painfully wide, Karwani scooted backwards across the sand. The apparition drifted forward, unhurried, her arms spread wide as if in supplication. His lips writhed with the effort of trying to scream.

She spoke a few soft words. They were in ancient Hebrew, vaguely familiar. But very ancient Hebrew.

Sound finally came from him. "Who... *what* are you?"

"I am Rahel, daughter of Laban."

"Not," he croaked, and swallowed. "Not... possible."

"No?" Abruptly she transformed. The mist vanished, revealing a girl his age, in jersey and shorts. The girl who had found him: Rachel. He was just about to breathe a sigh of relief when the mist returned, and with it the apparition.

"Is this the more possible? It is Yahveh whom I serve, and have served since first I was placed here in Zelzah. I was told to look for others. I was told to look for you."

"F-for me?"

She extended a hand to his and tugged. "Come."

Karwani had no choice but to accompany her. She had a physical hold on him, but did not harm him. He might have freed himself from her. But the other hold... he *had to* know. Even if no one would ever believe him, he had made a find. But a find of what?

Now it was this place, this cave, that was im-possible. He had heard, of course, of spirits of the land. People had lived and fought and died here since time immemorial. It was not unreasonable to suppose that something of them remained. Rahel was evidence of this, given that she was real and not a hallucination brought on by heat and thirst.

"I am," she said, "and it is not."

She drew upon a wall of scrolls, and selected one. Carefully she unrolled it. A snap of her fingers created a spark of light that hovered over her shoulder, so that she might see the words. "Do you read, John?" she asked.

"If that is ancient Hebrew, not well."

She began at the bottom of the scroll. "Simon was—"

"My father's name is Simon."

"Yes. He was begat by Yanis. Yanis was begat by Adlai. Who was begat by Malachi. Who was begat by

Ira."

Confused, Karwani shook his head. "I know all this. It is my genealogy. It is kept at home."

"It is of course incomplete," said Rahel. "The record of your lineage passed from physical existence in a pogrom during the reign of Ivan IV, the Terrible. The only male survivor of your family recorded a Semyon..."

"Who begat Zachry," said Karwani. "You said 'physical existence.' What else is there? We have the Torah, we have the Nevi'im, and the Ketuvim."

"Yes, the sacred books and writings. But there is also the history. We are the most literate people in history, John. We have kept a record of ours, from the very beginning. Our story goes back farther than any other. While many of our records have been lost to the predations of time and of other peoples, we as a people are most aware of all that has transpired. My task is two-fold, John. First, it is that of a connector."

For a long moment she gazed at him with the fondness of a doting maternal aunt, before shifting back to the scroll. "Sagiv begat Semyon," she went on. "There is an entire lineage here. Your lineage, John. There are many names, many," she smiled, "begats. Some of them are more significant to you than others. I give you four. The first two are: Terach began Shimon; Shimon begat Jonathan. The second two are: Muppim was begotten by Benjamin; Benjamin was begotten by...Jacob and myself. You are a Benjamite, John-Wadi Karwani."

A chill that had nothing to do with the temperature ran through Karwani. He had listened, but he had not understood. The difference frightened him.

"All these scrolls," he said, and did not know what to ask.

"I think you know very well what I am doing, John-Wadi Karwani."

He realized he did know—or at least could make an educated guess. The knowledge disquieted him further. "The urns... ashes. The scrolls..."

"Yes." She floated closer, and so did the spark of light. She continued to weep. "The People of the Book, if you wish. This, the land of Canaan, given to us by Yahveh all those millennia ago, is our homeland. It is where we belong, where we must come back to." In slow motion she waved her arm at the walls. "These have already returned."

"The Exiles?" he asked. "The Babylonian Captivity? Is that what you mean?"

"I have received direction from Yahveh that I will do this. I will bring home the remains of the descendants of those who were taken by Nebuchadrezzar to Babylon and who remained there even after Cyrus released them. As I have brought you home."

"B-but... I am already home. I live in Israel, in the West Bank."

Her beatific smile added to the glow from the spark. A gesture of her arm indicated the hole from which she had extracted the scroll of his lineage, as if to say that this was his home.

"But these people are dead, cremated," he argued. "I am not dead. I-I don't understand..."

"It is as it must be. I am unavoidable."

"No!"

Karwani turned and fled from the chamber and made a mad dash for the light at the end of the cave. He could feel her ghostly breath at the back of his neck. No doubt her arms were extended to embrace him and stop his progress. Yet he felt no touch on his skin, no sound in his ear save that of his own panicked breathing. He dared not look back, lest he suffer the fate of Lot's wife. Reaching the tumbled rocks, he scrabbled up them and into the daylight. Liberated from the sepulcher, he spilled down the rockslide and onto the sand of the riverbed.

Sunlight immediately began to bake him. There was still no shade. He had left his backpack and canteens in the chamber. The bicycle was gone. His gaze drifted to the sprawling settlement of Geba. It looked to be but two kilometers distant. Hope rose within him. He could make that, without water, even in this temperature.

He glanced back at the opening, half-expecting to

see the tendrils of a wraith. Nothing there moved. Even so, he did not resist the impulse to get up and run. As he rose, a sharp and hot pain in his right calf made him drop back to the ground. Another pain followed, this time in his left shoulder. He turned his head, already knowing what he would find, despite its desert camouflage: a sand adder.

Even as he rolled away, it struck once more, burying its three-centimeter fangs into the muscle along his spine. Then the serpent slithered into the shelter of the rocks.

The shock of the bites was as debilitating as the venom itself. He flopped back against a boulder. What matter scorpions now? He closed his eyes against the sun. There were no options. Hastening to Geba, assuming he could make that distance, would only hasten the effects of the venom. Calling out for help was useless, and would exhaust him further.

"No balm in Gilead," he laughed, his throat already dry.

The sun was a flatiron against his skin. The heat matched that around the bites he had received. His heart was racing now, whether from fear or due to the venom, he could not say, and it did not matter which. His head swam.

Presently a crunch of stones made him open his eyes.

Rachel was standing between him and the sun. Her aura of light might have come from the sun or from Heaven. He thought that she should be wearing a white robe, and not a jersey and jean cutoffs. She retained the beatific smile she had worn in the chamber.

Her mouth moved. He strained to listen to her fading words.

"You are home, Exile. It is as Yahveh has directed. I am unavoidable."

Yūrei of a Yatai Chef
Jessica Federle

Darkness—umami—
soy sauce rippling
around the moon,
a fat steamed dumpling.

I taste
night.

What thought
as I died
bound me here? What wish

keeps me wandering
these quiet streets,
legs as wheels of mist?

To feed,
be fed, perhaps to—*ah! Irasshaimase!*

Kyaku-sama, how hungry you look.
Sit. Eat—pork broth
suits the cold evening.
Talk with me awhile.

Others will join us soon.

Wild Darkness
Paula Cappa

The ghost beneath the hickory trees is a woman. She appears as a shivering presence among the leaves drowning in the summer sun. Her name is Falling Water. And she promised to show me the secret of death.

Few people here know about this mystery of dying. There is an art to it, I suppose, to die well. Will I be conscious in that final moment? Will I cease to breathe or will I be free of breath? And after, is there life after life? Or do we all just degrade back into the unconscious earth forever?

"Death is our eternal companion," so says Falling Water. She believes in dying fearlessly and has told me that souls *"journey to the southwest"*—although I'm sure she wasn't suggesting Texas.

In my latter years now, I've become stuck on the meaning of death, what the dark sages call the *evening cloud we all carry.* Falling Water understands the secret to dying, I'm certain of it. If Falling Water does not arrive soon and keep her word, I shall come to a bloated, stinky end and might wind up a splattering of nothingness in eternity. So, I wait for her in this odd but familiar silence in my little English country house surrounded by woods and rivers and wildlife.

At the moment, the main thing is being alive. Breathe in, breathe out, like the heartbeat of time— think, eat, sleep, rise, and do it over, day upon day. Some call it fruitful monotony—but honestly, the solitude has grown heavy now. I have few acquaintances these days; most family have passed, friends gone too. My old cat Jazzbow is dead, and the three before him. I've maintained the same face for decades, my skin worn out as a heavily creased glove.

"A well-finished death is a gift," Falling Waters had told me one fine summer day. She has the wisdom I

envy. Will she come now as promised, all sun-bronzed, and sit down with me, feathers hanging over her caftan, beads nesting in her fiery hair?

From my backyard hickory trees, a few leaves drift in through the open window. A sudden downwind hits my face. The wind often precedes Falling Water. So I wait, a rocking-chair cliché by the open bedroom window. I refuse to be old and small, sunken into an enormous bed of crocheted quilts.

Today my wall calendar is marked at September one. I breathe more slowly these days. Congestive heart failure. I will not see another September birthday. Falling Water knows this.

"We die the death we earn, my dear Agatha Ashfield." Falling Water prefers the sanctity of my full name. I like that. She frequently quotes White Elk about death: *" 'On the day you were born, you cried. A lovely babe. And the world here rejoiced. On the day you die, the world will cry with your departure, and you will rejoice.' "* She told me this at our very first meeting under the hickories. What could I, then a girl of only ten years, understand of that?

That was the day I fell into the Mohawk River while walking the slippery rock banks. Rapid waves slammed me down. I don't like to remember. The weight of the water. Gasping at the fading sky. Sinking into the dark. I do like to recall Falling Water's sturdy arms pulling me up, pushing me to safety as I choked up water. And I recall those kind eyes that so quickly faded from my sight, but never entirely left me.

I sit here, my vision fixed out the arched window on the row of hickories—shag-bark hickories with gray trunks split and furrowed like peeling paint. They have a talent to gracefully bend to thunder storms instead of resisting like the young oaks. I love such dignity. *"The hickories tell their secrets to Father Sky. And to Grandmother Moon and Great Earth Mother,"* Falling Water liked to say. I remember her storytelling days of the *Three Sister Trees.* I made her repeat this tale all through my teen years because I adore birch trees.

"Very long ago, three birch trees chose to live in a darkened field. The vivid darkness thought they were quite lovely sisters. Then the oldest birch bent over and died. The two sisters wept for days and then they also died in the creamy darkness. In the spring, a new birch tree decided to grow in the field. She thought about being the tallest tree in the forest and grew so high she poked a hole in the sky. Father Sky was pleased and pushed the sun to shine through the hole. And every field, mountain, and valley grew sister birch trees forever and forever."

At this moment, I am anxious to see Falling Water's liquid face staring out from my hickory trees. Her eyes, like drops of tinsel, find me on every birthday. My brother had insisted Falling Water was a childhood imagination, but I knew she was a real ghost.

"Falling Water. Where are you? Do you hear me calling?"

Outside, the air grows loose.

Falling Water loves the willful wind because she knows how to slip inside it, just like the blackbirds with white-tipped wings who glide within the breezes. She knew the ancient blackbirds when they were all snowy white with silver feet. She insists that Egyptians and Romans knew them, too. They interpreted the presence of blackbirds as revelations on the will of the gods. Augury. The art of ornithomancy is lost now. No one watches the flight patterns of birds or ponders their peculiar landings. No one asks why they draw circles on the sky or understands what secret unity makes them soar together so perfectly.

Maybe they are a bridge to the spirit world. If so, might we intuit their messages? Birds' oracles and omens go unnoticed in the modern world. So says Falling Water.

On my thirteenth birthday Falling Water told me to feed the birds and watch for a white-tipped winged blackbird. Of course I did and still do feed the birds, but I never saw a blackbird with white-tipped wings. One time one of them made direct eye contact with me.

I asked Falling Water what that meant.

"Blackbirds see you so that you will see their wisdom. Eight blackbirds crowning a treetop foretell a destiny, Agatha Ashfield. See them fly over Mohawk River."

Foretell a destiny, how deliciously mysterious. I vowed to watch them fly their circles over the river. I love the Mohawk River and greet it every day. In my younger years, I walked its banks daily, even in winter with mounds of snow and icicles, the trees sheathed like a fairy world.

Today the river is swift. I hear the grinding current. I used to think the waves were speaking to me but could not catch the words. These days, I seldom see the blackbirds making brave circles as they do at the end of every fat and lazy summer. But I know the flocks are flying high in pretty spirals. Last year a blackbird nested in my garden shoe inside my potting shed. A blessing!

"Are you coming today? Falling Water?" A heap of bronze shadows surge under the hickory leaves. I catch the flashes in my sight, but the shadows quickly fade. Is that the aroma of her sweet grassy smoke? Is she nearby? "I am here, Falling Water. Right here!"

"Your death lives inside you, like a splendid peach pit." Falling Water always had something curious to say to me. She died a virgin at the age of nineteen in a Mohawk village back in the 1600s. Smallpox. She told me her bones were buried during the Feast of the Dead. Now she wanders the green earth, alive in her ghost world. Falling Water chose to be a ghost of herself, something I fail to understand. What's it like to be a ghost?

Lucky for me though, because on every birthday my ghost beneath the hickories gives me gifts—dream catchers of feathered nets and fish bones, nut shells with rabbit fur, hickory bark and moss. A blackbird feather tipped white. And Falling Water's little prophecies.

The front door rattles. That's likely the Southwest Wind knocking again. Lately, I hear him nearly every morning at this same time. He's rather shy and would never push open the doors in my house. Not that Falling Water requires doors to enter. My stone house is set far into acres of woods, leaded arched windows and doors—my mother used to say *a little bit British*—with the walls in vintage flowery wallpapers: violets dress my sitting room, sunflowers in the kitchen, abundant blue wisteria in the bedroom.

I grew up here at Hickory House with my mom Victoria Ashfield—London-born, American-raised. At age twenty, I became a plain lady with a baby. I loved that man for one glorious night. He left when the winter winds blew over the river. My daughter grew up with me here. I named her Violet because violets are heart-shaped blossoms that grow hugging the earth. Violet became my rocking-chair baby—the gentle swinging never failed to soothe her. I still sit in that Windsor oak rocker with the bow back.

The front doorknob hammers suddenly. I think of an intruder with coarse dirty hands flipping the latch, skulking the windows to see if the house is vacant. What's here to steal? No cash that's for sure, although I do have a worthy pearl ring from my mother that's hidden inside a shoebox. Or, he's skulking to see if I'm alone. I hug myself, arms tight around my chest to keep steady.

On last year's birthday, Falling Water showed me the death shawl. She waltzed into my bedroom wearing a white and purple cape with yellow lightning jags, and spun around.

"Agatha Ashfield, you shall know this shawl, when the last day comes."

Singing a mountain chant, she danced brilliant circles. First wide circles then small ones. Taking the darkness from the room, she splashed the circles with fiery colors. Magnificent whirling. I remember how my breath dropped. I swore she was breathing for me.

After Falling Water left, her mandala dance-prints remained on the wooden floor. The colors lasted for days. Even now I can still see remnant specks along the wood grain.

Do I hear footsteps outside? Like boots thumping the flagstone. My mouth goes suddenly dry. I swallow hard. *Shhhh,* I make slow steps to the kitchen now. What if I see a man on the landing? I squeeze my eyelids halfway to peer out the window. No one is there. Silly fears. The bright morning sky invites me outside.

I hobble out to the back porch, sit in a sunny chair with my coffee and last piece of corn bread. I hear the Mohawk River slapping its feet. How soothing the sound. A tinge of smoke loiters on the air. Burning sage, grassy warm. Falling Water is nearby. Spirit and magic in her smoke. And her wisdom. But why should she give her wisdom to me, anyway?

"Death is the child of beauty."

Falling Water's words still haunt me, especially today. I want to ask her, how is death a child?

The far willow tree shivers. I watch it for a long moment. My garden is a wretched sight. Instead of upright blossoms, the beds are now a slum of weeds. What kind of gardener am I if my own family home isn't a showcase of florals and color? I spent my occupation as a floral horticulturist, my hands in the dirt for decades, talking to seedlings, fondling the blooms in so many garden centers and nurseries. The lure of soil, roots, stones, and sun hooked me every day.

Today, I have a perfect blue sky. If only I could touch it. Would it feel like silk? Beyond the distant mountain in the wilderness, white-tailed bucks are dropping their antlers now. Autumn on the way—they know what's coming. Deer often strut along the Mohawk River. Unlike me, deer are excellent swimmers.

Monkey flowers have grown out of control on the river bank now. I want to feast my eyes on their scarlet and yellow faces, but I am too weak to rise up and make the long walk. My old path is overgrown with sweet dandelions—*Taraxacum officinale.* I close my eyes and picture the Mohawk River. Walking upstream toward the source. A marshmallow morning with a pink sunrise. The small waves and their silver tarnish, ever moving. Just me, the river breaking, the hickories laughing, shells of hickory nuts cracking beneath my feet. And bird song, always bird song. What heaven is better than that? If there is a heaven.

I feel a squeeze in my chest. My legs are swollen again today. "Death is just another moment, right? Falling Water? Like falling to sleep? Into nothingness? Falling Water, please come!"

Slowly, I gather my strength and return to my sitting room with the violets on the walls. Sweet pea violets, all loose and free—*Viola odorata.* I sit down and realize I failed to close the kitchen door. I'm a milky-brained old sheep. My health aide, Martha, comes in the afternoon to prepare my meals, although I'm cert-ainly capable enough to manage a cup of instant coffee and put two slices of bread and a piece of ham together. I've even been successful at opening a can of soup—my daughter would be proud if she were still among us. A mother should never have to bury her child. Death struck Violet at age forty-eight. That dreaded phone call that all mothers shudder to even think about. The accident gave me no time to be with her. She died alone in her car. For Violet's sake, are there rocking chairs in heaven?

I decide I'm too short of breath to limp my way to the kitchen and back so will leave the door open until Martha arrives. What harm will that cause?

I hear a door crack from the far side of the house. The cellar door? Yes, that smack of the hinges when it opens. "Hello? ...Who's there?"

I hate this cold silence. Maybe it was just a hawk squawking? I imagine the intruder poised on the cement stairwell. Is that a knife in his back pocket? He's desperate. I can tell him about the pearl ring and then he'll be gone. What would he want with an old woman like me anyway? Oh, and my grandmother's silver teapot, the fluted Sheffield. Will that satisfy him?

I fight off a twinge of nausea and urge to cough. My heart is thudding now.

Bang! I lean over the arm of my chair to get a view of

the hallway into the kitchen. *Whoosh. Bang. Whoosh.* Falling Water would say it is wind magic, but this doesn't sound friendly. I gather my courage, rise up, and hobble to the kitchen—cane in hand, ready to strike.

"Ah-haa." A blackbird flutters inside at the window by the pine table. He beats at the glass and lets out a screech that shakes my bones.

"You poor little jailbird. Come along." I grab the newspaper and fan the air to direct him toward the open doorway. He's having none of it and cries out with violent flapping. Diving from ceiling to floor to window to wall, his left wing extends up, his right wing dips down. If he would only land for a second, I might be able to shoo him out. But no, he keeps whirling and now he is stabbing his white beak at the sunflower heads on the wallpaper. One by one, he hits the yellow petals with absolute precision. Intentional, I am sure, for he does not rip the green stems. *"Sunflowers model us to stand upright, be bright, be courageous,"* says Falling Water.

With every wild screech, his black feathers swell, throwing a darkness across the kitchen. Even the window light is smothered. I tremble, rub my chest— the thickening is tremendous. I am covered in shadows, deep as night. I cannot see a thing.

The blackbird is suddenly at my neck. His waxy claws surround my throat. I stumble back, clutch the bird tight... tighter... pressing my hands, crushing it until it releases me. With little breath, I scream and hurl it to the floor.

His withered wing flutters across my toes, and then stops. The bird lies dead at my feet.

"Agatha Ashfield." Falling Water's voice washes over me.

The relief that she is finally here makes me want to burst. She wears the death shawl. The fabric glows just a little, feathers pointing downward across her chest, her hair streaming out like a starburst. I want to fall into her arms but she is too far from me. "Do not fall away, dearest. Remain on your feet."

I reach through the dark for the pine table to support me. "I... haven't much breath."

"Be calm."

"Falling Water... so... this is... death?"

"The river does not run backwards, does it? Breathe in the earth's air, the same air drawn by all humans, creatures, and plants who live here. Take three breaths. Above all, remain conscious of yourself."

"There's... not enough air here."

"There is, the earth breathes with you. I breathe with you."

"I... can't grasp it."

"Focus on your inhale. Then let go. Step lightly, my dear."

"Too dark. I cannot... see ahead."

"The creamy darkness is thin enough to enter."

"It is not!"

"Agatha Ashfield, reach down and take the blackbird."

I reach down to my foot and gather up the bird. Cup it in both palms. The frail body holds so much sorrow. Bones like dried straw. I am filled with pity. "I killed it."

"Perhaps you have."

"Make it live again? Please... Falling Water, make it live."

"If you want it to live, release it."

I open my hands and it falls to the floor with a thud. I listen for it to flap its wings and fly away. Who made this awful silence?

"What shall I do? I've... killed it."

"Agatha Ashfield. Go to the hickories. Savor them. Feel the leafy stems inside you. Smell the sap and the skin of the bark. Get inside the roots among the rich soil. Become the hickory tree."

My chest is swimming with pain. I shut my eyes to remember the hickories. Again the silence. "I don't... know how."

"Then become the sweetened dandelion puffs along the river bank and scatter yourself as the wind blows them."

I picture the wispy heads. "I can't."

"Be the fringe on the fern. Become the branches weaved into the bird's nest. Be the bee buzzing inside the flowers."

"Show me! How?"

"I have no power to show you. Which do you choose to be?"

"I don't know."

"Yes, many die uncertain. Can you glide into the Mohawk River and become a single wave? Can you roll inside the water wisdom?"

"I... don't know water wisdom."

"Do this then. Bring the blackbird to your heart."

Blindly, I reach down. I sweep the floor. On my hands and knees I create circles. Overlapping circles, front and back. The floor is bare. "What shall I do? I cannot find it."

"There is only one choice left."

"Yes?"

"Permit the wild darkness to take you."

I have no strength to even cry out at such a thought. Let the darkness take me? Into the abyss? I have always trusted Falling Water. I cannot recall a single moment when I had cause to doubt her. Consistently wise, generous, loyal, and affectionate. Falling Water is *my* ghost. She promised me the gift of death. And here I crouch, like a child afraid of the dark. Who else is here with me except for Falling Water? And the blackbird, dead somewhere out of reach.

"Take my hand, Falling Water?"

"I cannot. Only you can detach. Permit the wild darkness to sweep you up."

"How?"

"Go inside the inhale. You owe Death one last breath, but no more."

Something quickened in my chest. "Wait."

Is there no turning back? To my Hickory House with the flowers? How I love to sit in my chair with the sweet pea violets on the wall. How I love to watch the last leaf fall from the tallest hickory like I do every autumn. I want to play with the monkey flowers. See the bucks by the river. I want to listen to the silence in the sunset.

"Falling Water, must I leave all this now?"

"The river does not flow backwards."

"I don't want death."

"There is no death, my dear."

"Then... what's to become of me?"

"You may become the wind and roll across the mountains with Father Sky. You may become the glowing energy inside Grandmother Moon shining through the hickories. I do not know."

"Tell me. Which is my destiny?"

"Maybe all of them. Maybe none. If you don't know, then you must choose the wild darkness."

"Is it safe?"

"Would I be here if it were not? Remain alert, my dearest. Be fully present. I will say it again. Step lightly."

I straighten up by holding the table. Inside the darkness, a soft breeze rises. I am in awe of its graceful power. I inhale slowly. A throbbing bubbles, fills my throat so hard it hurts. The hammering takes all my air. I shrink into a wild flutter. Someone calls me. Not my mother. Not my brother. Not my daughter. More like the voice of water. Is it the Mohawk River? I am floating. Drifting like a leaf on top of a curly wave.

Remain alert.

I step lightly.

A rim of the universe opens. I see Falling Water hiding her face amid a band of stars above Earth Mother alive in blues and greens. She sees me here. Her call is like a bell ringing into my body. I am a soaring black-and-white avian inside Father Sky. White-tipped wings, drops of tinsel eyes, feet like silver. I am weaving loops into endless figure eights with a flock of blackbirds above Mohawk River.

Who will watch us now? Who will see us quicken the world?

Look up, see our left wings point to heaven. Observe

our right wings sweep the earth. Follow our whirling wings as we print our message on Father Sky.

Will you see our rapid eyes, our uncurled feathers as we perch atop the hickory tree? Will you understand? We are a coronet, seven onyx beauties and me, affirming to all our conscious immortality.

Just as a barge enters Kaelennar, the city is attacked by an army of bloodthirsty esch. To protect fourteen-year-old Maelen Saltbearer, Gannet dresses her as a boy, and they take refuge with another family. Maelen wants to fight—she has some untested magical powers—but instead the children are to flee the city.

The occupation of Kaelennar continues, and the children eke out a meager existence, unable to better their lot against the esch... until one day Maelen Saltbearer is caught, along with her friends, while smuggling children from the city. Tortured and left for dead, Maelen snaps. Torn between personal revenge and saving her people, Maelen has a decision to make...

Available at www.irbstore.co
Or use the order form at the back of this book!

The Trip
Mark Towse

The face isn't clear, but I know it is my Rebecca—brown curls falling across the shoulders of her white summer dress. I can't make out what she is saying—it's as though the voice is playing out in slow motion and some notches deeper. But it's her. She is crouching down and running her hand tentatively across the yellow floor. I'm just a spectator in this—standing afar and watching the scene play out. She has no idea that I am here.

I don't know where we are, but it's the same place it brought me last time. Everything is blurry, and we are surrounded by moving shades of green—possibly foliage. I think she is crying. Her hair is blowing in the breeze, but I don't feel it. There it is again—the shift—the same time as it happened before. The greens are darkening behind her, and that smell again—a putrid cocktail of rotting vegetation and something burning. My skin is beginning to crawl, and blood is pounding in my ear with almost unbearable volume. Something is approaching her, and I know it to be evil—I can feel the oppressive malevolence it brings. And suddenly the blackness is punctured by a pair of bright red eyes, accompanied by a guttural rasping that fills my head. Rebecca looks up, and for a moment—I am sure we connect—and I hear myself scream for her to look behind, but then she continues to scan the patch of green beneath her.

My heart thumps aggressively liked a caged animal, and the familiar dizziness is beginning to wash over me—helplessly, I can only watch as the ominous black cloak begins to wrap around her. She screams, but it is distorted and distant. And slowly, she begins to fade away behind the black curtain.

I am losing connection—the darkness is quickly

working its way towards me like a tide coming into shore—and now I am sinking into the ocean of black. It is just me treading water now. But I know better than to fight, and just let it take me—

"Jon."

"Thirsty!" I reply.

A glass is shoved into my shaking hand, and as I clumsily gulp the water down, some of it splashes on my neck, snapping me back into reality quicker than usual. Finally, the shaking begins to subside, and my heart rate slows, but I feel depleted—heavy and disoriented.

Her friendly smile is a welcome relief.

"So?"

"Nothing more. It's too hazy—ambiguous."

"Damn!" she replies. "I thought this would work."

"Did you try it?" I ask.

"No, but the guy said it was strong stuff—has been used for hundreds of years. To be honest, Jon, I think I've had enough. I'm getting strange dreams since the last batch. And I've just started getting these—well—visions. They just creep up on me throughout the day."

"Visions of what?" I ask, putting my socks and shoes back on.

"Bad stuff, Jon. Dark. We are not supposed to be messing with this world. How do we know these visions are the truth and not some twisted version induced by the evil that inhabits the in-between? Each time I come back—I get an icky feeling—as though some of it returns with me."

I know what she means.

"So, that's it? Are we done?" I snap. I know it comes across as harsh, but I can't stop now.

"Let the police do their job, Jon—this isn't the answer."

"Do their job? They have found nothing, Amy. Three months—and nothing! Everyone still thinks it was me. They dragged me through the dirt—hours of interrogation when they should have been out there looking!"

And I watch her face crease, and her eyes begin to

glisten with moisture.

"I'm sorry, Amy. I just—"

"I know, Jon. I know."

I'm an idiot.

The familiar lump of anger and sorrow swells at the back of my throat, and it's all I can do to fight back my tears.

"What was he like, Amy? Your son, Jake—if you don't want to talk about him, I understand."

It's the first time I have asked, which is crazy really, but my head doesn't have room for anything else. I have wallowed in the grief for so long that I have forgotten about the rest of the world.

"He was nice—smart, quiet, but intensely sad," she said. "As a parent, it's hard to watch, but when he met Rose, things changed."

"Is that the girl with him in the photograph on the mantelpiece?"

"They bought a house, made plans—even talked about having kids. But she broke his heart, Jon. Said it wasn't for her and she left him. It crushed him— surrounded by memories and promises. He moved back in with me and, well, you know the rest."

"What about Rose? Where is she now?"

"Someone told me she was in Italy—took off with some other guy. He always thought she would come back to him—insisted on keeping the pictures up—and I haven't had the heart to take them down. There's even a pair of shoes in his room. It's bittersweet for me—she gave him his happiest days, but also his saddest."

"I'm sorry, Amy. It must have been hard to watch."

"This stuff, Jon. We know so little about it—the long-term effects, etc.,"—making her wish to change the subject very transparent.

"But it takes me so close, Amy. I can't let go of this. I am not sleeping. I rarely eat. The only thing that helps is the drink, but I don't want to become one of those. I'm not here, Amy—this is not living."

She leans against the kitchen sink and eyes me with sympathy and compassion—but with a subtle difference to the ones I am used to—less generic and delivered with an understanding that only those in the know could project. She exhales deeply, shoulders dropping and eyes moving to the floor.

"I have something, Jon. My conscience is telling me to keep it a secret, but I can't bear the grief in your eyes."

"Please, Amy—I'm desperate."

"I don't know much about it, Jon. It comes from even further in than the last stuff. More powerful—purer. The tribes use it to not just to speak with the dead, but to touch them—it's their last chance for them to embrace the relatives they didn't get the chance to—before they disappear from the in-between to the next life."

"So, I could touch her. Feel her?"

"These are rumours, Jon. I don't know how true they are—word spreads from tribe to tribe. I haven't summoned the courage to try it."

"I need it."

She looks at me with a furrowed brow, but she knows better than to try and talk me out of it.

"I feel bad. I only wanted to try and help, but I feel as though I am dragging you into something."

"I'm a grown man, Amy. You gave me hope—it's the only thing that has kept me going. Don't take that away."

"Come back tomorrow, Jon—you look exhausted," she says, placing her hand on my shoulder.

I know she's right. It's the middle of the afternoon, but I feel as though I could sleep for days. We embrace and maintain the hug for some time. I have only known this woman for a few weeks, yet we have been through so much—both our lives turned upside down with grief.

"Okay, I'll bring the doughnuts and coffee—you supply the drugs."

She eyes the picture of Rebecca on the inside jacket of my wallet as I count out the payment. "She was very beautiful." And the past tense is lost on neither of us. Before she has a chance to say anything else, I smile and give her a final pat on the back.

Reality assaults as soon as I step out the front door. Everything is so defined, and the sharpness of sounds is startling—the birds, the cars—yet it feels even more distant than the middle-land.

Melancholy is like a disease—it spreads throughout your soul until it possesses you—and it has me beat, under its sombre spell. I know Rebecca would not approve of this. Hell, six months ago I would have mocked such spiritual mumbo jumbo, but I have seen what I have seen, and there is no going back.

Amy and I met at a grief-counselling session. After visiting the apartment one day and catching me asleep on the couch next to an empty bottle of whisky, Rebecca's sister recommended I attend. Amy and I lasted one session and after that we sort of counselled each other, albeit with no previous experience and a shit load of hash.

The apartment is cold when I arrive. Summer is well and truly over, and I flick on the heating after throwing my coat across the couch. "On the rack, Jon,"—her voice utters softly in my head. And I pick it up and place it in its rightful place next to hers.

Every time I get home, there is a rush of adrenaline—a small glimmer of hope that she will be here. But I know she is gone—why else would she appear in these visions? The malevolence I observe around her in these scenes is taking me down a dark path, and I get the feeling she is only hanging on for me—that she already has one foot out of this world.

I get one of the ready-made meals from the fridge and place it in the microwave. The next part of the process involves filling a tumbler half-full of whisky and drinking it before the timer goes, then refilling it and retiring to the couch with my food. I think about turning on the television, but the remote is on the other chair. Reaching out, I grab the small block from the coffee table and crush some of it into the marijuana before rolling the joint—usually the last part of the routine before I retire to bed. I look towards the clock and decide to smoke it anyway—there are no rules for me anymore.

It isn't long before I feel the effects. The warmth is beginning to fill the room and the internal heat from the whisky is bringing on the heaviness, and—

I am here again. The grass is yellow and dry, and the birds are whistling their summer songs. It sets the scene for our last day together, and it's one I have relived so many times.

And there she is.

Rebecca places the blanket onto a patch of grass in the middle of the clearing, and as we sit down, we both wince as the sharp grass pierces through the thin material. And then we laugh. It's odd. I remember the conversation—rather the monologue by Rebecca so vividly, yet I was half-listening at the time. I was distracted—my head full of project deadlines and new ideas I wanted to implement at work. Six years I had been an architect at the firm, working all hours and finally making partner—but it took only two months for them to cut ties after her disappearance—a big climb up, but a massive drop waiting on the other side.

I hear her now, though. She has my full attention as she speaks about her colleagues and clients, and all the exhausting politics and socialisation of running an advertising company. My wife was a force to be reckoned with—black and white, you could say.

—*Was a force*—

And there it is—the moment she sensed my disinterest—the eyes projecting her disdain. I knew at the time that I had been caught out. I hear the feeble and predictable word leave my lips, "Sorry, I was—"

It was too late; the damage was done.

"Are you smoking that stuff again?" she scowls. She is on the assault now, "I can tell, Jon. You have that stupid vacant look—"

I know it's just a dream, but I can see every rigid line in her face with remarkable clarity. All I can do now is watch helplessly once again as she stands and brushes her summer dress down. "You promised!" she utters, before dramatically tugging her wedding ring off and throwing into the long grass just outside the clearing. She marches off back towards the car, and I am left standing there—the picnic is over. Countless times, I have watched her walk away.

My mouth is dry as I wake, and the dream feels like a dream now. But the emotional journey it takes me on each time leaves its mark. She gave me the silent treatment all the way home. Like a child, I festered in my anger and frustration at not being able to do as I please. We got home, I dropped her off and drove to the office—a real dickhead thing to do.

It was perhaps two or three hours later that I returned, and this window of time is something the police have questioned me about on many occasions. The vagueness of my answers did not help, but I was smoking a lot—time slips through the net sometimes. The house was empty—no note—no indication that she had left. I found her phone on the kitchen table—that was a worry—she never went anywhere without it.

My first thought was to return to the picnic area, but there was no sign of her. I tried to find the ring but had no luck. I rang her friends, then swallowed my pride and rang her parents. But nothing. She had vanished.

It's hard to describe the feeling—a mixture of helplessness, abandonment, and regret—but also a detachment from anything else that was going on. My mind was full of Rebecca, and there was no room for anything else.

I walk over to the sink and gulp some water from the tap. The clock tells me its 4 pm. There is no way I can wait any longer, so I grab my coat and march anxiously to her house.

"Amy!" I shout, knocking on her door.

I hear footsteps down the hallway and the door swings open, "Hey, Jon. I was expecting you," she says—a nervous smile on her face.

She switches off the television and walks over to the corner of the room, lifting one of the floorboards. "This one is expensive, Jon. Six times the normal rate—it's bloody rare!"

"Sure, I'll sort that tomorrow," I reply, knowing that is more than the last of my savings.

With undeniable poetry, she adeptly prepares the liquid and pours some into two bowls.

"Are you coming along for the ride?" I ask.

She is agitated—her hands are shaking. "I've done nothing but think about it, Jon. It scares me, but I don't know how else to find any peace. I want to hold my boy one last time."

I place my hand across hers and smile. "I'm nervous, too, Amy. But if it gives us answers—"

She reaches for her bowl and drinks the liquid, before sitting back into the chair and closing her eyes. I grab mine and guzzle every drop—I need this to work. After removing my shoes, I sink back into the couch and can already feel the transition. This stuff is good.

Spiky grass beneath my feet—I can feel it, and the breeze and warmth from the sun wrap around me. Leaves rustle gently, and the air—it smells like summer. I am in the clearing where we had the picnic, but I'm present this time. I am here. The sun's position—it's late afternoon.

Rebecca.

Her white dress floats in the breeze as she walks over to the long grass—shoes in her right hand. She drops them next to her, before bending down and brushing her hand across the brittle hay-like grass— just like the visions showed me.

"Rebecca!" I call out, but she does not hear me. I rush towards her—and—I can feel the ground beneath my feet and the breeze through my hair.

There is another voice then, not hers—in the distance. I am running as fast as I can, but not gaining much ground. And again—that voice—not sure if it's male or female, but it's getting closer. I still cannot make it out.

No sign that Rebecca hears it either as she continues to search the grass for the ring. She looks frantic now, urgently moving from one patch to the next. I can hear her sniffles and impatient breathing, and a wave of grief and guilt washes over me. Did she die here, looking for her wedding ring?

The ground still rushes beneath me, but the distance is closing painfully slowly. The promise of contact—a final embrace, brings a tightness to my chest—I would give anything.

Suddenly, the sweet smell of summer is giving way to something else. That familiar rotten smell is permeating the air, and the hairs on the back of my neck warn me that something evil has arrived.

Something moved behind the trees—just then, I am sure of it. The ground—once hard is now soft and my feet are sinking into it as I try to close the distance. The air is becoming thicker around me, and the light summer breeze suddenly escalates into a gust, blowing directly into my face.

Sunlight is fading rapidly—but I see it—a shape moving between the trees. And then that voice again, coming from the same direction, but so distant. It still isn't getting clearer.

And finally, behind Rebecca, someone emerges from the shades of brown and dark green.

"Rebecca!" I scream.

The temperature has dropped, and I can see my breath in front of me. This place—so different now. Oblivious to the stranger behind her, Rebecca continues to search the grass. And as the stranger approaches, she momentarily hovers her hand above the grass—for a moment I think she must be aware, but then I see her shoulders drop after pulling something from the ground—it must be the ring. She wipes her face, stands, and brushes herself down, before putting her shoes back on.

A strained scream leaves her lips as the stranger's arm wraps around her neck, snapping her head back. She is being dragged away, back into the darkness— legs kicking in protest and hands flailing at the arm around her throat. I have never heard my wife scream before—it's a terrifying sound that curdles my blood.

"Rebecca!" I shout again, helplessly. Desperately.

It feels useless—my heart wildly thumps as I continue to scramble through the darkness against the wind. The soft ground beneath is starting to give, and my feet are sinking deeper with each step, as though the ground is trying to swallow me. My vision is becoming intermittently fuzzy—in and out—and my head is pounding and swimming with dark shades of brown and green. No—not now! Not now!

I hear more muffled screams as I finally reach the first tree. Doubling over, I lean against the bark and begin to cough violently—and as I suck in the thick and pungent air around me, I immediately vomit a lump of dark viscous liquid. Already, I have been here too long.

The voice floats across—it's getting close. "Please, no more!"—undoubtedly, a female cry.

Over there—one of Rebecca's shoes—on the floor. And then the other. And as I step from the shadow of the trees, I see her body lying across the ground, clothes matted with blood—she is crying, and through a pained rasp, I hear my name, "Jon."

Crouched beside her, holding a knife, is a man that is familiar somehow—but I can't place him—he is whimpering, and I can hear him spitting words out under his breath. He looks up then, and a sudden look of shock creases his face. I am sure he can sense my presence.

And then it clicks—the guy from the photo. It's Jake.

Rushing past him and scrambling to the floor, I wrap my arms around my wife. I feel her—shaking, terrified—but I feel her."

"Rebecca," I whisper.

"Jon, is that you?"

"It is me, love. I'm here. I'm so sorry," I utter. Overwhelmed, I begin to cry like a child—relentlessly and uncontrollably. She is back in my arms. As I bring her in close, she lifts the ring inches from the ground, and I wrap my hand around hers. I feel her breath on my neck.

And then I don't.

"Why did she have to leave, Mum?" the stranger sniffles.

I turn just in time to see Amy approaching from the darkness. *It was Amy that he could sense, not me—her voice floating across the darkness.*

Our eyes lock momentarily, and then she averts them back to him. She saw me, though. I know it.

But now I feel myself slipping—everything is swimming away—a blur of opaque colours merging into one—I am—

Alone—back in Amy's lounge. My throat is as dry as the desert. Rushing to the tap, I grab at the handle and take in huge gulps of water—the taste of vomit still in my mouth and the oppressive thickness of the air from the in-between still clings to me. In my right hand, I can feel the ring—it's warm.

It came back with me from the middle land!

Amy is still under—most likely embracing and saying goodbye to her murderer son. Did she know? She mentioned the visions—the evil they conjured. Is that why she stopped?

I take the opportunity and rush up the stairs. There is one door closed—it must be his. As I push it open, I am confronted with walls full of photographs of Rose— almost every square inch filled with a sinister montage of adoration. More pictures of her adorn the bedside table and some bottles of perfume that no doubt, were hers sit atop a desk. There is nothing overly suspicious. Against the far wall stands a large dark wood wardrobe, and I rush over and open the door—to find the bottom shelf crammed full of shoes. The second pair belongs to Rebecca—the ones she wore for the picnic. And for her death.

"Jon," Amy's voice behind me—distressed.

"Did you know?"

"Of course I didn't, Jon," she says. Her reply is firm, but not as stern as I would expect.

"It got too much—it's why I stopped." She looks

down towards the ground and begins to cry.

"Go on," I murmur.

"I just wanted to know why he killed himself—how he was feeling at the time. The visions showed me the darkness that had started to embrace him—the hopelessness. He appeared wrapped in a black smog—like a cloak. At the time, I just thought it was inner turmoil—his depression at losing his only love—and that it had carried over into death. And then the vision took me into the bathroom next door, and I watched as my only son slit both his wrists with a Stanley knife—his face expressionless as the water turned pink around him. His eyes were bright red, Jon. Bright red. But I never thought him capable of murdering anyone. You have to believe that."

"But you must have seen something else? Some clue?"

"I didn't, Jon. Only—"

"Go on," I utter.

"The shoes. I—I didn't think anything of it at the time. But—well—at first, there was only one pair in the cupboard. I knew them to be Rose's as I remember her wearing them. But then others started appearing, too. I just thought—perhaps—I don't know. I blanked it out. I didn't want to—" and with that, she begins to bawl and slide down the wall—arms around her legs as though trying to make herself as small as possible.

"You think there are more?" I say, trying to process all of this.

"I saw them, Jon. All five of them. He took them to a field and buried them. One of them was still alive as he shovelled the earth on top of her."

"How do—he told you this?"

"I saw, just now in the vision," she replied. "I saw all of them die, Jon."

"How did he know? That Rebecca would be there, I mean."

"He told me everything. It was the drugs. They were showing him—and he was doing so much of the stuff. I was feeding his habit, Jon—trying to keep him happy, distract him from—but you must believe me—"

"What do you mean the drugs?" I yell, patience wearing thin.

"There is evil in the middle-land, Jon—spirits stuck in eternal damnation that are neither here nor the next life. And they watch us—and wait—for new souls that they can twist. They sensed his weakness, feeding his insanity and hatred for women—filling him with so much darkness that it had to come out sooner or later. They told him they had also been let down—hurt—cast aside by those that once loved them. Over time, they befriended him and worked him—told him that all women were mocking him, laughing behind his back—fuelling his rage further. They lead him to her, Jon—told him she would come back for the ring. And he waited, in the trees."

"This is crazy—too much. We need to go to the police, Amy."

There is a knot in my stomach, and I'm hit by a wave of dizziness. This woman—this pillar of support that I think of as being a best friend—her son murdered my wife. What am I supposed to do with that information?

"Why, Jon? It's done now. Rebecca and Jake are dead. What would be the point of going through all that again?"

"The other women—they will have people that care—like me. They deserve answers. Closure."

"But, Jon, I can't go through that. It will kill me—"

"Amy, I am not asking—this is something you must do!" I scream at her. She recoils and withdraws back into her ball. I don't know if I can handle this. I can feel the adrenaline surging through my body, and I want to grab her shoulders and shake her into the realisation that her son was a cold-blooded murderer.

"He is still my son, Jon. I held him and nursed him as he cried on my shoulder. He is sorry—for everything. He is."

I have just witnessed my wife's murder. Consoling this woman should not be my job.

As I squat down next to her, I am still gripped with anger, but as soon as I reach for her hand and stare into her watery eyes, cannot help but feel pity. Confessing is the right thing to do—for me and the others. I stand up tugging on her arm and reluctantly, she gives and gets to her feet, and we make our way towards the bedroom door. As I pull it open, the red eyes are the first thing I see—framed by the swirling cloak of darkness. I don't feel any pain, and it's not until I look down that I see the knife jutting from my chest—the crimson stain developing across my shirt.

The black cloak surrounding Jake works its way slowly around me, and I can feel its heaviness beginning to weigh me down.

"I'm sorry, Jon," Amy says from behind me. "But I was afraid you would react this way. It's why I brought him back."

The darkness continues to cocoon me until I can no longer move. Suspended in its oppressive thickness and too weak to fight, some of the black fog begins to seep into my mouth and nostrils. I see the darkness coursing through the veins in my wrist—and I feel it—the iciness as it takes hold of me. My vision is filling with black ink, aggressive swirls that are slowly stealing my sight of this world.

My body is shutting down—leaving this world—for another place.

He is taking me back to the middle land, I know it.

I will find you, Rebecca.

Edited by H. David Blalock

[Phantasmagoria is a Victorian-style theater troupe based in Orlando and St. Louis. They practice interactive theater, playing on the natural human fear of and attraction to the paranormal. The St. Louis show, held on the Mississippi riverboat, The Becky Thatcher, explores globally-known ghost stories and weaves in the city's rich history of unsettled spirits, leaving the audience wondering which ghosts still walk the St. Louis streets. I attended their show in November, 2019.]

Aboard the Becky Thatcher
(A review of Phantasmagoria, St. Louis, Missouri)
Koji A. Dae

One by one we step across the straining plank
thirsty for explanations
behind a century of pain
baked into weathered bricks

Autumn mist creeps down the current
glimpses of white pinafores beckon us
crinoline beneath crimson
weeping to be heard.

Below, we rock to a lullaby of fractured spirits
those burnt
abandoned
lost

Boot heels on the bottom of the boat
echo muddy river sorrow
one story broken
into five voices

The sadness of St. Louis
whipped to a peak
then released
in a smoke of phantasmagoria

The New Job
Damian Jay Clay

From the top of the hill the light was still good enough to see the silhouettes of the larger and more elaborate gravestones at Kilmaine. A fine mist was building up into a fog and obscuring every other part of the surrounding view.

Michael Sullivan wheezed his way along the hard mud road that led from the bog back to his cottage, pushing a wheelbarrow in front of him. It was filled with the wood he'd collected after a day of bog-cutting. He'd left the sods of turf out on the ground to dry—the effort of a hard morning's labour, and left his slane resting next to the peat it had cruelly hacked from the ground. There—another load to bring back in a week's time.

Recently, such journeys grew harder every day. Years ago, he would tell everyone it was what kept him so fit, but now, and he would admit this to no one but himself, it was becoming too much. June was approaching and the turf cutting season would soon turn into the hay cutting season, bringing little relief.

The east wind battered him as he reached the top of the hill. A sharp pain climbed his right knee as his foot caught then slipped over a half buried stone—he let go of his load. The cart had found its way to the decline and rolled out of control, accelerating for a few seconds before it veered and overturned, emptying the wood onto the hard ground.

He stumbled over to the wreck, pushing through the pain which tore all the way through his body. As he collapsed next to the broken cart, the rain began to fall. He looked up and screamed out in defiance as the simulated tears of a lesser man fell down his face. As the pain in his body became almost intolerable, he realised he needed a new job. He was just too old to dig turf and push such loads any longer. He could barely manage the rest of his smallholding. Then pain left him along with everything else.

In his dream, he slipped back to the year after he had just been married. Mary had made two bowls of scrambled eggs and set the table for breakfast before the sun had come up. She turned up the paraffin lamps, which bathed the kitchen in a reassuring straw glow, then shovelled up the coals from the hearth on which she had been cooking, throwing their remains back into the fire.

They sat supping at the eggs and sweet tea, alternately dipping their toast into mug and bowl.

"We were up to dig the grave for her last night," he said. "I suppose the burial will be tomorrow."

"She'll be watching the graveyard at Kilmaine. Ah, God love 'em Mick, but shouldn't the family be taking care of that?" Mary rested her hand on his. "Jesus knows you're busy enough."

"Well, all she had was Sean, and God knows he's too old for digging. I spoke to him last night—the house collapsed, the wife dead, the children emigrating years ago. He doesn't know if it's yesterday or tomorrow."

"Does he have no relative to go to?"

Michael shook his head.

"Where's he going to live?"

"You wouldn't believe me if I told you."

"Go on..."

"He spent the last two nights on a chair in the wardrobe in the half of the house that's still standing. Says he won't move. Thinks the wardrobe will protect him if the rest of the house falls in."

Mary looked at him wide eyed; she was waiting for a reaction, any reaction.

He held his straight face.

She burst into hysterics.

The branches above him creaked and found harmony with the low bassoon note of the wind against the trees. A familiar old face shook his hand and wished him luck, then walked away down the road. Who had it been? He couldn't place the man.

It was dusk and the first day of his new job. He stood at the the entrance to the graveyard and looked out at a misty Knockroghery evening. He could barely make out the lights from the nearest cottages. The sound of a donkey-led cart coming down the Tallowroe Road left him wondering at the identity of its unseen owner. They'd be lucky to make it home before dark.

There was an old wooden milking stool on the right side of the road. He sat down and closed his eyes, letting the night pass without him.

In the morning, the birds sang from high atop the trees. The earth smelt damp. It must have rained overnight. He stood up and walked around, looking at the gravestones. All the familiar names were there: Curley, Donnelan, Finneran, Connors, Giblin, Fallon, Macklin. He'd been here for many of the burials.

In the fields below, farmers were out cutting hay. As the day went on, a man came down the road driving his cattle, no doubt to market.

The day went, and another night—day and night, and day and night again. How long would he be working for, and how did he ever got this job?

It was an evening in the winter. The nights were drawing in. He stood by the great oak in the centre of the graveyard when he heard two young boys play-fighting their way up the road. He stood behind the tree and listened in on their conversation as they stood just outside the cemetery.

"Will you go in then?" said the red-headed boy.

"It's your turn for the dare," said the blond boy.

"It's not!"

"It is! I went and got the apples from Gilligan's orchard last week."

"There could be anything in there!"

"Will you go in or not?"

"I will. How far will I go?"

"To that big tree."

The red-headed boy nodded, then took a deep

breath, as though he was about to dive into a lake. He paced stealthily for the first few steps, probably for the fear of disturbing anything that might be living or dead. He began to shake as he got further in, then suddenly started running towards the tree.

Michael came out from behind the tree and shouted at him. "What are you doing in here?"

He screamed and ran back, only to fall over a broken gravestone. He picked himself up and sprinted away, his scream in unison with the friend's who'd waited for him at the entrance. They both ran back down the hill together, shouting and cursing.

He'd lost all track of time. Had he been here months or years? He didn't know.

For a long time he'd seen no one at all. The only company he'd had were the birds, and an occasional fox or squirrel. The human visitors to the graves had stopped coming further back than he could reckon.

Then one day, from far off outside the graveyard, came the sound of a car engine, men shouting and ordering one another around. Minutes later, two gangsters dragged a blood soaked man into the graveyard. They were followed by husky man in a black leather jacket who was carrying a pistol.

Michael hid behind a gravestone and looked on.

The two men threw their victim to the ground.

"Kneel down!" shouted the man with the gun. "Keep facing away from me."

"Please, Jesus, I beg you, don't do this to me."

"Say your prayers." He raised the pistol up to the man's head.

"Our father—"

Bang.

They were there an hour. Digging a shallow grave and burying the poor dead man.

That night, he stood watch again from the old chair. He kept looking over to the new grave; he couldn't keep his mind away from it.

A distant bell rang as the moon reached its zenith.

He was pulled out of the graveyard by an unseen force, back towards the entrance. He turned to see the shot man rising out of his grave. Michael knew he should have been terrified, but didn't feel any such thing. He didn't feel anything. Even the cruel Irish wind did not chill his skin. The poor man walked towards Michael, and not knowing what else to do, Michael shook his hand, and wished him good luck.

Michael turned and walked towards his home, but as he did so, the world around him began to fade against a bright light.

It was only then that he thought back to a story he had heard as a child. A story about the graveyard at Kilmaine that his father had told him after the death of a close uncle:

"Death really isn't the end, Son. But when someone dies and is buried at Kilmaine their ghost has to watch the graveyard until the next person comes along. It's the last duty between life and death."

His service was now over and it was time for something new. He hoped that wherever he was going, he would once again see Mary.

Sub-Rosa
Benjamin Whitney Norris

A mind left open is the end of the world,
where all these roads have led us,
and beggars line the road,
begging for a way—to move on
from the bones of saints and martyrs
to the world-building intellect,
the demiurge. To move out
into His deepest channels, then;
in rain-soaked cardboard boxes, carrion.
Even His body has been integrated
in a matrix, inhabited by creatures
not unlike ourselves, our cells,
our cloister, beatific and magnified
by His unholy lens. Here, illuminations
gestate and give birth to a black hole
burned in parchment, last night:
a paradise for symbiotes and collaborators
to strive for, to succeed, to be mindful
of all things
lacking attribution.

Road Trip Buddy
Trisha McKee

The dreams were always so real. Carly could feel the pain of her nails digging into her palms, could smell the sour stink of her childhood home, and she could taste that metallic in her mouth, the taste of fear.

These dreams were different than normal dreams because Carly was always in control. Not in the surroundings or actions of others, but in her own thought process and reactions. She was always standing off to the side watching, as if it were a movie and not a chunk of her past replaying in front of her.

Carly had left her childhood home ten years ago, at the age of seventeen. She had walked away from the abuse and craziness, the neglect and toxic environment. She said goodbye to her mother's tirades, the endless men, and the brutal beatings that left her scarred both inside and out. She had put herself through college with scholarships, grants, jobs, and loans. By age twenty-three, Carly was employed at a prominent company writing manuals for government procedures and machinery.

By age twenty-seven, she was well-established as manager of the technical writing department. And while her career thrived and her social life was adequate, Carly rarely dated. The thought of giving up any freedom, any part of herself to a man was terrifying. She got her fair share of offers, even as she tried to play down her looks with minimal makeup and only the necessary fuss to her chestnut brown hair. Still, guys sometimes mistook her icy nature for playing hard to get, a challenge. It was only after several stern refusals that they got the hint.

Carly had no contact with her family. Not her mother's side, not her father's side. Not a sibling, not even a twice-removed cousin. Her friends filled that void. When asked about her past, her childhood, Carly said as little as possible. Not to keep secrets, but to keep that past from roaring back into her mind with memories and emotions she was not capable of handling. She had barely survived. She had barely crawled out of that war zone.

Life was full. Carly's heart was full despite that past. She had made it. And she had pushed all those memories aside. They distracted. They destroyed.

So these dreams were more than inconvenient. They were pulling at the strings of her comfort... of her sanity. Carly wanted nothing more than to continue marching forward as if there was no past. These dreams sucked her in and left her in a daze for days, her mind taking and dissecting the details, the people, the dialogue... the memories.

The dreams had started about six months ago. The first one had shaken Carly to the point that she had called in sick to work, and she had sat on the couch, tired but afraid to sleep, shell-shocked over what her mind had shown her. If she had not been asleep, Carly would have been positive she had time traveled.

A month later, she had another dream. This one brought to her mind a person she had completely forgotten about, on a day she had pushed out of her mind. The sheer intensity of the details convinced her while she was in the dream that she somehow traveled through dimensions. Because this was not a dream.

She was standing outside of her childhood home; a rusty, leaky trailer. She could smell the sulfur from the paper mill, could feel the breeze, and she saw her mother standing there with a man that Carly remembered was her boyfriend. Not her husband. Her boyfriend.

Her mother and the guy were fighting. He was demanding she leave her husband. Her mother was wearing that yellow and gray top she wore around the house. Carly had forgotten all about that shirt. Her mother's blond hair was long, over her shoulders, down to her waist. She was beautiful, more stunning than Carly had remembered.

"That your mom?"

Carly turned. There he was again! Griffin. He was her coworker. A guy she really knew nothing about, had little interaction with, and could not understand why he was showing up in these spookily real dreams! He had nothing to do with her past.

He had appeared in the first dream, but he had hung back, both of them shuffling their feet awkwardly as they tried to figure things out. But now he was beside her, watching intently.

"That's her."

"You have her eyes. Without the crazy look, of course."

Was it that obvious that her mother was certifiably insane? Then she reminded herself that this was her dream, so of course anyone in it would know. She would project her memories, her thoughts, onto them.

"Yeah. This—they fight and then mom's husband comes home unexpectedly and... well, he always has his gun on him. He holds them hostage in the house. I get home from school, walk in the house, and right into this. We're there for ten hours until he finally lets the boyfriend go. And mom, mom tells me that he must really love her to do all that. When the boyfriend reports it to the cops, mom denies everything. Says her husband would never do that and the guy is just jealous. Makes me lie, too."

She could feel Griffin's eyes on her, that is how intense the dream is. "Did he hurt you?"

Unable to voice it, she shrugged. "It was so long ago."

"That means yes."

"Hit me to shut me up but that was nothing new. Mom's boyfriend got it a lot worse."

As soon as the words were out of her mouth, that old run-down car she knew all too well sped past her and Griffin, screeching into the dirt driveway. Carly jumped back and instinctively grabbed Griffin's arm, feeling flushed and relieved when his hands steadied her.

"It's just a dream," she insisted with a nervous laugh. "Why am I so jumpy?" But then she dropped the pretenses. "I don't want to see this. I can't... do this again."

Before she could see Griffin's reaction, she felt herself stumbling down a long, dark hallway. Then she was inside a house with towels for curtains and folding chairs tucked into a wobbly, chipped table.

"Griffin?" Carly was not sure why she assumed he would be there. Perhaps she thought by controlling the dreams, she could control his presence. But why? They had barely spoken more than a few words to each other in the years they worked at the same company. Sure, she found his stoic presence powerful, that long dark hair and beard masculine, and his physique, those calves alone had her practically drooling. But she had not realized the extent of her crush until he materialized in her dreams.

And if she could control her dreams, why were they in this dirty shack that she did not recognize?

"I'm right here."

His deep voice sounded off, so she turned and studied him, noting the paleness of his skin and the clenching of his fists.

And suddenly it hit her. "This is your house?"

"House? If you can call it that. It was one of many places we stayed." Then his eyes widened and she followed his stare as a beautiful but frazzled woman rushed into the kitchen.

"Laura, just watch him for a few hours. I gotta work tonight."

"Mom, you don't have a job. You're going to Jimmy's and getting high."

The woman stopped and pointed at the pouty girl who was also attractive but had unwashed hair and dirty fingernails. "You watch how you talk to me. Seems you're the one that can't keep a job or be clean for more than an afternoon. I'm asking you. We need groceries. We need to stay here. I have to work."

Carly turned to Griffin, who was staring with a

blank expression at the scene before them. "This is the night that when my sister leaves and I'm alone—I think I'm around ten—one of my sister's junkie friends breaks in and ties me up, roughs me up, and steals everything. And..." he turned to Carly, his lips curled up in a semblance of a smile that contradicted his shadowed eyes, "I was blamed fully for that."

It seemed that before Carly could react, she was waking up, her head full of clouds from that trip, that dream. Her body protested any type of movement, begging for more rest, but her mind and spirit were racing. What was that? Was it her subconscious simply allowing suppressed memories to slip through after all this time?

Carly felt like she was moving through a haze, that dream overtaking her thoughts, overwhelming her, so that work was almost impossible. Her focus just was not there. She was both fascinated and traumatized over the re-surfaced memory. For years, she had shoved the memories down, ignoring, denying, refusing. For years, she had forgotten. And with one night, one dream, it had all come back to her.

Something, Carly assumed it was curiosity, pulled her over to Griffin's desk. He sat hunched over, working on some code, not acknowledging anyone that called out a greeting. He was nicknamed Gruff, because of his somewhat abrasive manner. He could be nice, was often seen joking around with others around the office, but when he was working, he did not want to be interrupted.

"What?" he growled without so much as a glance her way.

Carly shrank back, any confidence whooshing out of her. "Uh. Nothing. I just... nothing."

He glanced up and sighed. "Sorry. Deadline. Did you need something?"

"No. I just wanted—was going to ask about a movie I heard you guys talking about earlier. Sorry." She turned, almost colliding with someone, and raced back to the safety of her cubicle. Later in the afternoon, she noticed Griffin walked past, his steps slowing by her cubicle. She squinted her eyes, as if studying something on her monitor, and felt her face flush, relieved when he simply continued walking.

It was just a dream. She probably placed him in her dream because she harbored the slightest crush on him. And that crush probably existed because he was unattainable. He was gorgeous and grumpy, and she was both fascinated and scared. He was not someone who would notice a woman that could barely get two words out without shaking. The only time she was confident was discussing work issues.

So when Griffin stopped by her desk at the end of the workday and asked her if she was going to join everyone at the bar across the street for happy hour, she immediately shook her head. That was too social, and she was not too fond of being around drinking. There was always one that could not handle alcohol and it made Carly nervous.

He nodded. "Yeah. Not usually my thing, but today's been a day of it." And then he was gone, leaving her in a puddle of uncertainty, in a tangled mess of emotions she had spent most of her adult life avoiding.

But as the weeks dragged on, Carly was able to compose herself and focus on her life, which was work. She worked, she slept, she ate, and one weekend, she met some friends for lunch. Another evening, she browsed in a bookstore. But then it was back to work, sleep, food. It was a safe life. It was a boring life that held no risk of danger, of relying on a person that could turn around and hurt her. Lonely? Sure. Safe? Absolutely.

"C'mon, Carly!" Joanne pleaded. "Just come out with us for a little bit."

"No, thanks. I need to catch up on some things." Her Saturdays were sacred to her. She did not want to be stuck with a group of coworkers bar hopping.

Joanne rolled her eyes. "What? Spending all day at the library?"

"That sounds like a perfect day to me."

Carly jumped and glanced up to see Griffin shoot her a brief grin before continuing on down the aisle, and she wondered if he had even spoken or if it was just another dream echoing through her exhaustion.

The following week, she had another one of those dreams. She found herself in that old living room with the tattered couch and wood-paneled walls. Her throat seemed to close up, and she gasped for air.

"It's just a dream. Carly, breathe."

She turned and tilted her head up, tears streaming down her face. Why was Griffin in her dream again? Why was he standing with her in this trailer that held her worst nightmares? Her most intense shame? "I can't do this. Why am I dreaming this?"

He slowly shook his head, his long dark hair falling around his beautiful face. "I'm not sure why we're here. But just remember it's a dream."

"I don't want to remember this. It took me years to forget."

To her surprise, he reached out and patted her shoulder. Carly only slightly jumped, but then her focus moved to her mother, so young-looking, slamming down the phone and screaming for her husband.

"That bitch's school called! Goddammit. I'm gonna kill her. She told them she was hungry. That nosey guidance counselor says she thinks Carly is also exhibiting signs of being abused."

Carly gasped, the memory of this day smacking her in the face. They had bombarded her at school and as a ten year old, she was not sure how to answer the questions thrown at her. Did she lie and cover for her mother? Did she trust these adults and hope there was a way out from the hellish home life she endured?

In the end, young Carly had trusted the school officials, only to find out she'd been wrong to do so. Because they told her mother everything she had confided. They poked her mother with empty threats, mere warnings, no intention of saving the young girl. Only going through the motions to save their own hides, saving hers the furthest from their minds...

"This is the night I get beat so bad, I can't make it to school for a week. I remember being so scared I'd never be able to breathe right again. My ribs were... I had a concussion too."

She could feel Griffin's eyes on her and then his voice coated her with a warmness, a comfort. "You jump a lot at work. I figured... I mean, I recognize the... I'm sorry. I know this is just a dream, and I'm projecting my own experiences... but I always wondered... And I'm sorry. If you were hurt. If this is anywhere close to what you went through. I'm sorry."

There was a long silence between them as they watched the scene in front of them, Carly being reminded of the pure misery she had lived through. Finally, she said, "I'm sorry too. If any of this is real."

Suddenly she straightened. "Uh, Griffin?" She felt his fingers wrap around her arm gently, comforting. "I have to go. I just... My younger me is about to walk through that door, and somehow I know I'm not supposed to be here....when I get here."

"Okay. Hey... do you mind... if I stay? I'm kinda curious about younger you."

Carly paused, strangely touched that someone was interested in that child, that forgotten bruise on society's record. But then she nodded and hurried out the back door.

And suddenly she was at a strange house where a little boy with dark hair and large, caramel eyes sat at a shiny, long table with an older man and a young-ish woman. She realized with a start that it was a very young Griffin.

"Son, please understand. This doesn't mean that I won't be your dad—"

"Actually," the woman cut in, "that's exactly what it means." She sighed when the man shot her a look. "C'mon, Bill. He's old enough. What is he—like, 10?"

"I'm twelve," the boy grumbled, his chin resting on his hands, his eyes cast down.

"Son, listen. Rain and I are getting married. I want to convert to her religion but to do so, I have to relinquish parental rights to you and annul my marriage to your mom. So that means, you won't legally be my son."

The boy lifted his head, his eyes wet, but his gaze solid. "Then whose son am I?"

The man stuttered around, seemingly taken aback by the boy's calm question and intense demeanor. "This is just a formality. I'll still be around. Griffin, I'll still come get you some weekends. You'll come here. Hang out."

Carly noticed that Rain did not look pleased at that, and Griffin did not look convinced. In fact, he sat back slowly, his gaze never dropping. "Right. Dad. Sure."

Exhaustion always plagued Carly after these dreams. She dragged through the day, usually trying to avoid Griffin, embarrassed that her subconscious kept bringing him in, even creating a storyline for him, a background to his character. Ignoring him was not difficult as he seemed oblivious to her presence.

But that cool attitude must have affected her because in Carly's next traveling dream, Griffin was beside her apologizing.

"I feel like I come across as... not the warmest person toward you. I want you to know, even if it is just telling you in my dream, that it is just... this is intense. You know? It's like we spend all night together, traveling to my past, to what I imagine as your past and then I see you the next day... I have too much going on to be knee-deep in these emotions."

Carly turned away from the scene in front of her, the dream-movie playing out and reminding her of all she had worked so hard to forget, and regarded Griffin with surprise. "Yes. You just summed it up. Well, my subconscious summed it up. I think that this, returning to my past... remembering the horrors of it all, I'm bringing you in to soften this."

"Why would I soften this?"

"Because." She realized this was a dream. It was safe to say what she felt. "I'm crushing on you, so to have you here as a comfort soothes over the rough spots."

He studied her for a moment, and Carly noticed the wild gleam in his eyes, as if he were contemplating something, mulling it over and over in his mind before—and suddenly his lips were on hers, his arms sliding around her, holding her up as she grew weak from surprise and desire. Carly had known she was attracted to the guy, but she'd never fully acknowledged the pure cravings for his nearness, his touch...

Suddenly he was pulling away, his stare just over her shoulder. "What's going on?"

She turned, remembering with a sinking heart that her most dismal childhood moments were still being played out. "Oh. That's when they came to remove me from the house. I broke my stepfather's nose."

"That guy there? He's huge. You're so tiny."

"Yeah. Panic will make you do some amazing things." She ignored his questioning stare. "When I get home, they take me. I have time to pack a small bag. Mom doesn't even hug me goodbye. She keeps telling those people that she doesn't understand how I turned into such a monster."

"So...foster care?"

"For a few months. Then I'm returned here. Back to this hellhole." She swiped at a tear, the roller coaster of emotions throwing her for a loop. To be thrilled by a kiss one second and then torn apart by a traumatic memory the next... she was overwhelmed. "I spent years forgetting this shit," she hissed, part of her anger coming from her display of emotions. "I can't understand why I'm remembering it now."

Griffin's hands fell onto her shoulders, this time out of comfort, not lust. "I don't know. I keep asking myself that. I think maybe because I've pushed it down anytime I remembered it... I'm finally having to deal with it. To heal. And I think I brought you into my dreams because you keep to yourself, you're jumpy. I assume you have a past that's... maybe I can relate to you more. And like you said, you soften this experience."

The dreams did not return for a few months. Carly

was beginning to breathe easier, to not toss and turn, afraid to go to sleep. She relaxed and again began pushing back the memories that haunted her. Things with Griffin were beginning to smooth over. Carly no longer tripped over words when having a conversation with the man. She understood she had simply dreamed some rather crazy dreams, bringing him in to soothe the rough edges.

"No, my dad met a younger woman and..."

Carly had approached the group of guys to ask Keith a question, but she stopped as Griffin spoke.

"...she wanted him to convert to her religion. That meant signing off rights to me, but the church wouldn't allow it. Said they just couldn't do that as he had been my father all those years. But I rarely saw him after that, so he might as well have signed away rights."

"Griffin." She spoke his name softly as the other guys continued talking, not hearing her, but Griffin's head shot up, his eyes wide as Carly's stomach jumped. "Griffin." She moved to the side, away from the others, and Griffin followed suit, leaning forward to hear her softly spoken words. "Your dad sat with you at the table, with his fiance when you were twelve to tell you what he was going to do. That he had to sign away rights."

The color drained from his face. "Carly, how do you know that?"

She was trembling but worked to keep her tone steady and strong. She needed him to hear every word. "I know because I was put into foster care after breaking my stepfather's nose."

His eyes were as wide as saucers, his breathing heavy, and she wanted to poke him, to help snap him out of the shock, but she was much too shocked to do any of that. Instead she felt her nostrils flare and her nails dig into her crossed arms as she realized what this meant. Those dreams...

Griffin turned and walked away.

Pack a Lunch
Robert J. Krog

Rebecca's eyes snapped open, and her arm was reaching over and smacking Tom on the chest before she realized what she was doing.

"What!" asked Tom, sitting up bleary eyed and confused.

She sat up, too, and said, "Sorry, I had a dream. The car's going to break down today, but I have a really good feeling about it, so it's okay."

"Oh," he said, slowly, rubbing sleep from his eyes. They sat there, waking up for a moment or two, wondering about the time, and thinking that going back to sleep would be nice, but not wanting to leave her statement about the car unresolved.

He turned on the lamp on his bedside table and asked, "Do you mean another vision or," he paused rubbing his face some more, "just a dream?"

"Sorry," she said. "A vision type dream."

"Oh," he said, and he yawned, shaking his head. "That sounds pretty inconvenient. I can't take any days off work. Do you know what's going to break on it? We could get straight to an auto parts store and fix it first thing before you drop me at work." He rubbed his hands through his hair and looked down at the alarm clock. It was four thirty. They should have been asleep for another hour and a half. Back to sleep was best, he thought.

She said, "I don't know, but I have a really good feeling about it breaking down. I think I should just pack a picnic lunch for us and roll with it."

"What? Seriously, I have to work."

"Not for all four of us, honey, just for me and the children. It's going to break down after I drop you at work." She let out a huge yawn herself.

"Well, I'd like to get home from work, too."

"I have a really good feeling about it. I don't think we

need to worry."

"You're only seeing a possibility for today, right?"

"Yep."

"And not even all of today?"

"Well, yes."

"Then, since having the car break down'll cost us money in repairs and time lost from work, why don't we just avoid it?"

"Because," she began again, "I have a..."

"Really good feeling about it?" he finished for her.

"Yes."

He stared at the love of his life, his wife of five years, at her round face, her sleepy, brown eyes, her disheveled, blond hair, her frame still plump with the baby weight from their second child, now an active, crawling ten month old. He trusted her, of course, but he still asked, because she had only just awakened, too. "What did you see that gave you the really good feeling?"

At some point in their conversation, she had taken his left hand and was still holding it. She said, "I saw me driving back home after dropping you off. I know, because it was still morning, and I was thinking about what to do with the day, and the children were in their car seats. There was a CD going. The Silly Songs CD was playing John Jacob Jingleheimer Schmidt. We were singing along. Suddenly, something popped, and steam shot out from under the hood. I pulled over on the side of the highway. I hadn't noticed the temperature gauge going up into the red, but it had. So I got out and opened the hood. Of course, I know nothing about engines, so I just left it open and looked around. You had the cell phone, so I couldn't call for help. The area was like a park almost, so I let the children out to play and waited to flag a car down. I wasn't worried at all. It was a beautiful day. Not too many cars come down that road anymore, but I figured one would be along eventually. All I thought was that it would be nice day for a picnic. Then I looked into the woods and saw the dogwoods blooming under the pine trees."

"Okay," Tom said, slowly, "I have an idea. We'll fix

the car anyway. It's probably a hose or the thermostat, or something easy like that. I hope it's not the radiator. Then you and the children can picnic out for lunch without having to be stranded on the side of the highway."

She mulled that over a moment then said, "Something was about to happen. If we fix the car, I might not stop at the right spot and then I might not be there for it to happen. Give me your cell phone, though. I'll pack a lunch, and I'll call your work when we break down, then you can have Chris or Mike drop you off where we are with the right part to fix the car after work."

He stared at her. She smiled at him.

"What if they aren't available? What if they have to work later than I do? What if..."

"I have a really good feeling about it, Tom." She stroked his face gently.

He stared at her some more.

"Trust me," she said.

"I do trust you. Why don't we stop by the parts store before work and get things ready, okay?"

"Two reasons."

"Oh?"

"One: how would you explain to your coworkers that we had the necessary parts already in the car? Two: I think timing is part of what will happen, and we should just keep to our normal schedule."

"Right."

"Roll with it," she said.

"Roll with it," he sighed, and turned off the lamp. "Let's get some more sleep."

They lay back down and snuggled together.

After a moment of snuggling under the covers in the dark, she asked, "Does it bother you that I came back different like this?"

"No," he said, matter-of-factly and sleepily, "it would have bothered me if you hadn't come back. This, we can handle."

"Okay," she said.

After a moment, he added, more seriously and a

little more awake, "I was scared to death when they said your heart stopped. Eight minutes. They almost didn't resuscitate you, and David was still inside you, waiting to be born. No, I'm fine with psychic powers. Being without you; that would be a bother, you understand."

"A bother?" she asked.

"A soul-wrenching agony," he affirmed casually.

"So, when you say 'a bother,' you're making a masterpiece of British understatement?"

"Yes, except I'm not British." Their legs were touching, because that was how they usually fell asleep. He reached over and took her hand.

"Right."

"Right."

She sat up, took his other hand, and put them both where she wanted them. "Kiss me," she said.

He did.

⟪∗⟫

They left for work at the usual time, packed into their economy car. They had a large throw blanket, water bottles, and a cooler with a picnic lunch stowed in the trunk. The children were buckled into their car seats. David was smacking enthusiastically at the toys dangling from the handle of his seat. John was making growling noises on behalf of his stuffed bear. Tom was frowning as he drove.

Rebecca said, "A mule walks into a bar and orders a drink..."

He glanced her way, "Yeah, and?"

"And when the bartender brings its drink he asks, 'So, why the long face?'"

He groaned. She giggled.

"I looked under the hood this morning anyway, of course," he explained.

"Traitor," she accused.

"I couldn't find anything wrong."

"One is a traitor for attempting as much as if one had succeeded."

"What's the good of you having premonitions if we don't take them as warnings?"

"I don't know, but I really have a good feeling about this."

"I don't see exactly why."

"Neither do I, but let's just roll with this one, like we agreed."

He sighed. "Yes, ma'am."

"You're only saying that, because you think you have no choice."

"Maybe, but disagreeing doesn't mean I don't love you or anything."

She folded her arms over her chest and harrumphed.

"Cute," he said.

"Don't call me cute when you won't believe in me."

"Okay. Ugly."

She smacked him on the arm as hard as she could. He laughed.

They drove on. She glanced out the window. The sun was low in the east yet, and the woods on either side were in shadow. Under the pines and oaks, she could not see the dogwoods and redbuds she knew where there. Absently, she reached her left hand over and entwined its fingers in his right. They rode in silence thus for the rest of the drive.

***

The parking lot at the mill was mostly empty when they arrived. Tom pulled up near the entrance and put the car in park. "Here's my cell," he said, handing her his battered, old flip phone. She took it and leaned in to kiss him.

"Going to work, Daddy?" asked John from the back seat, when their lips parted.

"Yep, sure am. This is the mill. This is where I work."

"This is the mill?" the boy repeated, looking around with interest.

Tom looked at his two-year old son and smiled, wondering why he was charmed by the way the boy had happily asked the same question every morning for the last two weeks.

"The sign," said John, pointing.

"Yep, there's the sign."

"Lights up," the boy declared emphatically.

"Sure does," Tom agreed. He looked Rebecca in the eyes and said, "Be careful."

"I won't be in any danger, sir. You keep your hands, arms, legs, and head away from those saw blades."

"Yes, ma'am," he said. They kissed again, and he got out.

"Bye, daddy!" shouted John, waving both hands.

Tom blew kisses before the door to the mill shut behind him.

Rebecca moved into the driver's seat and put the car in gear.

"Silly songs!" John shouted.

She smiled and clicked them on. It was a fine morning. Feeling eager for the adventure, she remembered to drive as she normally would, in no particular hurry, back toward home. The sun was a little higher, and its beams were shooting down under the forest's canopy when the CD filled the car up with "John Jacob Jingleheimer Schmidt!" Somewhere in the third repetition, there was a sudden, loud pop, and steam started shooting out. Sure enough, she hadn't even been looking at the temperature gauge, but it was in the red. She slowed and pulled over into the grass.

"Mommy?" asked John.

"Yes, dear?"

"Where are we?"

"We're on the side of the highway, honey. We have to stop the car."

"Play?"

"In a minute or two. Let me pop the hood and have a look." *As if,* she thought, *my doing that will do any good.* But she pulled the lever, stepped out, raised the hood, and looked. It was hot. There was steam. She shrugged and looked around. It was a beautiful day.

The area was like a park. In fact, she thought she saw a concrete picnic table or two back in the woods a little, and a spot a few yards away that was actually paved for parking. She hadn't noticed it before, because it was mostly covered by dirt and pine needles.

"Mommy? Play?"

"Sure thing, honey. Let's get you out of that seat." She unbuckled him, and he climbed out, bear in tow, to explore the grass by the road.

"No, honey, stay on this side of the car." She reached in and lifted the lever by her seat that popped the trunk open. From his infant seat, David was beginning to fuss. She went around and lugged the blanket out. She spread it before retrieving the baby. He happily rolled off into the grass as soon as he was on it.

As she picked the cooler out of the trunk, she glanced up and down the highway. No cars. She looked into the trees. Under the pines, there were dogwoods blooming. She smiled. Anticipation thrilled in her stomach. John was running in circles in the grass. She unloaded the trunk and moved everything further into the shade.

They played chase, sang songs, collected pine needles into piles, threw pinecones about, and generally had a rollicking good time. David tried to eat everything he could get his tiny hands on. The cell phone rang around ten. It was Tom, of course. She had forgotten to call him.

"So, my love, how's it going?" he asked. There were shrieks of metal tearing wood in the background.

"We're playing in this old, abandoned park."

"Just like in your dream?"

"Yes, but we're past the dream now."

"Did you see any loose hoses?"

"Nope, can't say that I did."

"Did you look?"

"Not recently. Guess I should do that, huh?"

"Please."

She went to the engine compartment of the car and looked in. After a brief consultation, Tom decided they needed a new thermostat.

"It's not terribly hard to replace," he said, "and it shouldn't be too expensive either."

"That's nice, dear," she said.

"Anything wonderful happen yet?" he asked.

"The dogwoods are blooming, and we're playing under the trees."

"Hm," he said.

"Love you," she said.

"Back atcha. Gotta go."

She put the phone in her pocket and went back to find David crawling toward the pavement. She snagged him and returned to the blanket. "Snack time," she declared.

It was later, after the snack, as they were drowsing on the blanket, that she looked up and saw the man walking out from under the trees. She sat up quickly and smiled uncertainly. The man was average in most respects; of an average height and weight, possessing an average face with brown eyes and hair. He was dressed in jeans, white t-shirt, and hiking boots. He had a stick in hand, a branch he had probably picked up in the woods. He stared a moment with a dull expression, then responded easily to her smile with one of his own.

"Hello," she said. Beside her, on the blanket, the children slept on.

"Car trouble?" he asked, glancing at her vehicle.

"Yes," she said. "Out hiking?"

"I was taking a walk. What seems to be the problem?" He walked toward the car.

"I don't know much about cars, so I can't say for sure," she said, rising carefully to avoid waking the boys.

He leaned his stick against the car and looked under the hood.

"I appreciate your concern," she said, "but we'll be fine."

"It can't hurt for me to look, if you don't mind," he said, glancing at her with a smile.

She warmed to the smile and returned it. "Sure," she said.

"Your kids?" he asked, glancing at the boys.

"They're mine, yes."

He looked back under the hood and asked, "What'd it do?"

She walked over beside him and looked in as well. "It overheated and blew steam."

"Oh," he said, and started poking around, testing the hoses with his hand.

"My husband thinks it's the thermostat," she offered.

"Oh, you're married," he said, not looking up. "That's nice."

She chuckled.

"Eh?" he asked, glancing her way, his brown eyes intent.

"I guess that is a legitimate response in this day and age. There're a lot of women who aren't married but have children. I was raised to get married first, so yep, I've got a husband."

"Hm," said the man looking under the hood, "Where's he?"

"At work," she said, adding after a moment, "He'll rescue us after. We were out picnicking anyway." She had a momentary thought that it might have been wiser to suggest he'd be right back, but dismissed it. The dream had given her a really good feeling about the day.

"Well," he said, "The hoses don't seem to have blown or anything. I think your husband may be right. Mind if I check your coolant level?"

"Go ahead," she said. He took a look and declared that she hadn't lost much.

He stepped away putting his hands in his pockets and smiled at her.

"I appreciate your looking," she said.

"No problem."

"So, are you just out hiking?"

"Something like that. Taking a walk. I haven't taken a walk in a long time, not like this."

"I see."

They stood a moment, looking at each other. She brushed hair out of her eyes and looked around. "It's a gorgeous day to be stranded, if one has to be stranded."

"Hm," he said. "It is a beautiful day."

"The dogwoods are blooming."

"Is that what those are?" He looked into the woods.

"Yes. Those smaller trees with the white, cross-shaped blooms." She pointed. There was a beam of sunlight falling on one, and the blooms seemed to glow. They enjoyed the view. He turned to her presently and observed—or asked, she wasn't sure—"It's nice being married."

She nodded. "Yes, it is. I really like being married."

"Your husband, he must be a good guy, a lucky guy."

"Oh, no," she said, "I'm the lucky one."

He smiled, but she noticed that the smile did not make it to his eyes.

"I have a pair of children myself," he offered, his eyes searching past her to the blanket on which her boys were sleeping on the grass.

"Oh. How old are yours?"

"I'm not sure, actually," he said, "I don't get to see them, and I've forgotten their birthdays. I'm not married to their mother." He smiled again the smile that did not reach his eyes. He picked up his stick and twirled it idly.

It flashed through her mind then that she was in a moment at which she could either stand awkwardly without saying anything or she could reach out. She offered her hand and said, "I'm Rebecca."

He blinked slowly and then extended his hand, "Ralph," he said.

"It's nice to meet you, Ralph," she said, shaking it firmly.

"Yeah," he said. They released and stood as before.

She said, "It has to be hard not seeing them. Are

you divorced?"

"Never married," he said, his smiled fading and being replaced by a more thoughtful or bemused expression. He was hard to read.

She chose from among a variety of options and asked, "Hard feelings between you and their mother?" The day wasn't feeling as good as the dream had indicated.

"You could say that," he admitted.

"I'm sorry," she said. "That has to be hard."

"I was raised to get married first, too," he said, regarding her with a steady, thoughtful expression, "but just didn't do it that way."

Was he challenging her about it, waiting for her to judge? What? "Okay," she said, "I think you're a nice man, Ralph. It's very good of you to see the hood up and check on us. A lot of folks might have gone on by."

He laughed, "A lot of folks might have decided to take some sort of advantage of the situation."

"True," she said, "But you haven't, and that's a good difference."

"I haven't helped," he said, gesturing at the car.

"No, but the thought counts for something."

"I see," he said.

She smiled.

"So there's nothing I can do for you then?" he asked.

"No, my husband will be along. You must have had a good walk already. I've got some water over there, if you'd like a drink."

He blinked slowly again and nodded.

She paced over to the cooler and took a water bottle out of it. It was still quite cold. She took it over and handed it to him. His face was very serious, but he said, "Thank you," and took a drink.

"I've got some snacks too, if you're hungry. There's enough to share."

He shrugged and drank. As he drank, she looked around at the beautiful day. Another man was coming out of the woods, this time from the across the highway. It was a sheriff's deputy. He was tall, middle aged, and in good shape. She smiled and waved. He was over both lanes by the time Ralph turned and saw him. Something passed between them that Rebecca couldn't guess.

The deputy said, "I thought I might bump into you out this way, Ralph. How've you been?"

"Oh, fine, fine. I've been out for a walk."

"Good day for it," said the Deputy, smiling all the way up to his blue eyes.

"You?" Ralph asked.

"Not bad. No complaints. I enjoy a good walk."

He turned to Rebecca. "Car trouble, ma'am?"

"We think the thermostat went bad. My husband will be around after work to rescue us."

The Deputy saw the children for the first time. "Well, ma'am, you don't have to wait that long. My car is on the other highway, about four hundred yards through the tree there. I can hike back and have you on the way home in about fifteen minutes or so, I guess. It'd be no problem."

She smiled. "That's kind of you, but not necessary. We came to picnic and play outdoors anyway."

The Deputy nodded. She saw that his uniform had his name on it; "Peterson."

"Well, you can call the dispatcher and get a hold of me that way, if you change your mind, Mrs...?"

"Rebecca Walker," she supplied.

"That's fine, then, Mrs. Walker," he said. He turned back to Ralph who was draining the water bottle. "Let's walk on that way, while we talk, shall we Ralph?" he suggested, "So we don't wake those little boys."

Ralph smiled another smile that didn't reach his eyes. He handed the empty bottle back to her and said, "You take care now, Rebecca."

"You too," she said, smiling. "You men be careful in the woods."

"Oh, we will," Peterson assured her. He gestured and Ralph tossed his stick aside and preceded him across the two lanes of the highway. Peterson waved as they disappeared into the woods.

She stared after them, wondering what was between the two men. It was odd.

The children woke up soon after. They had more to eat. The boys played the afternoon away and were tired and ready to go home when Tom arrived in a pickup with his coworker, Chris, who had a tow chain. He pulled them home, Rebecca and the boys riding with him, while Tom rode in the car. Chris and Tom spent the rest of the afternoon fixing the car. The problem was only a little more complicated than Tom had thought.

It was later, after the children were in bed and Tom was in the shower cleaning the grease off, that the phone rang.

"Hello," said Rebecca. "Walker residence."

"Mrs. Walker, this is Officer Peterson. I had the office find your number. I hope you don't mind. We met on the side of the highway noonish today, if you recall?"

"Of course, I recall, Officer Peterson, and I don't mind a bit. What may I do for you?"

"There are two things ma'am. I wanted to be sure you'd gotten home, and that seems to be the case?"

"We're just fine."

"I'm glad to hear that."

There was a pause, and she filled it. "Officer Peterson, I'm wondering how your friend, Ralph, is doing. He seemed like a nice man but a bit down on his luck or maybe depressed."

He laughed, "I wouldn't call Ralph and myself friends. He's the other thing I wanted to talk to you about. Got a moment?"

"Go ahead."

"Ralph escaped from the county pen this morning. When he ran into you, he was on his way to murder his ex-girlfriend."

"Oh, my God," she said, and she sat down on the side of the bed. "He was going to murder her?"

"He said so, Mrs. Walker. This is not conjecture."

"Right. Wow. Oh, my God."

"Invoking the Lord in a thankful way wouldn't be inappropriate. I'm sorry to tell you this, but I think you should know. He said when he saw you, he was planning on robbing you and perhaps murdering you as a prelude to murdering the girlfriend, sort of a workout, maybe as a way to figure out how to do it. He was wondering if he had it in him to kill the boys, too."

"I... What?" Her mouth went dry, and she suddenly had nervous energy in her hands.

"That's right, Mrs. Walker. But he didn't. He couldn't really say why, but he said that something about you made him change his mind on it. He was quite sure he still wanted to murder his ex-girlfriend, but he figured he wouldn't harm you."

"Oh, thank God."

"There you go. Anyway, if you hadn't been there, and hadn't impressed him that way, I think I'd have found one or two sets of bodies around the county today. It was a good thing you were there when you were, or he wouldn't have been there for me to find. I'm glad it went down that way. He was distracted, and by the time he saw me, I was too close for him to run. He knows I would have shot him, and I'm a good shot with a pistol. So, he went quietly, and that's a good thing. Nobody got hurt, and hurt sure was what he had in mind until he met you."

They talked a little longer and then she hung up after saying, "Thank you."

She sat on the edge of the bed. From the boy's room, she heard one of them make a noise in his sleep. In the shower, Tom was starting to sing. She sat thinking. That was not how she had thought the day would go. She'd had such a good feeling. She stood up and began to pace. Tom was singing a hymn. She checked on the boys then went back and sat on the bed again.

A few moments later, Tom stepped out of the

shower, drying off and still singing. She hadn't filled him in on everything that had gone on. She began to think about how she would, for she kept nothing from him.

"Well, it was a good day," he said, getting dressed.

How to answer that? She thought of Ralph's ex-girlfriend and children, still alive. A thrill of relief suddenly went through her.

She said, "Yes, it was."

An Angel Sat Crying
Stephen Abel

Walking alone
Wanting blue skies and a sunlit day
Rain mixing with tears
As both run down my cheeks
In a race away from sadness

hoping to find something
Though I knew not what it was
An answer maybe?
But what truly is the question?

The park
Was desolate and abandoned
No leaves to blow
Had there been wind to blow them
No animals to feed
Had I crumbs to feed them
And no one to tell about the things
I did not see

Then, I saw Her
Feathered wings drooped around Her
Crouching on a pedestal
Where the shattered statue behind Her
Used to rest

I approached
To inquire as to
Her melancholy posture

She looked up, glassy-eyed
And wiped softly with Her thumb
From corner to corner across
The lower lid of my eye

"Angel," said I, softly and calmly, "shouldn't you be
smiling?"

Her sobbing paused
as She collected Herself

Then, speaking weakly in a broken tone, She asked,
"what's there to smile about?"

"Should I," said She, "smile about Hate?"
"Or war?
Or maybe famine?
How about greed, gluttony, or lust?
Persecution, poverty, or perhaps
Abuse, rape or murder?
Disbelief, disease, or depression?
Lack of morals or lack of education?
Maybe crime?
Or its lack of punishment?

"Tell me," said She, "what should I smile about?"

"Love," said I

The Girl in the Basement
R. Michael Huberty

Some people hunt ghosts. You see them on TV with their electromagnetic field detectors, digital voice recorders, and thermal cameras. They're looking for a voice that will croak their name on the audio file or a blob on the camera that they can Rorschach Test into a humanoid figure. They're looking for proof of the afterlife. They want to meet the "other side" in person.

On television, it all looks pretty exciting, you're constantly seeing people who say they're grabbed or see a shadow in the corner, usually just before the camera can swing over to get the shot. They seem to be able to pick out full sentences from deep growls and static, and when you're seeing the subtitles right before you hear the clip, it's a miracle, you can seem to understand them, too. But those shows are days of investigation edited into a 44 -minute "greatest hits" of the whole endeavor and half of the show is a replay of something you've just seen or a preview of something you will see in a minute. It's only the best moments. Nobody wants to watch a show where nothing happens. That's called life and it's boring. That's why we watch TV.

In reality, paranormal investigations are a lot of walking around places that are freezing (investigators often talk about cold spots, but when nobody is paying for the heat in an abandoned building, everywhere is a cold spot.) An investigation is hours of sitting in a place waiting for something to happen and asking questions in empty rooms. And for all of your efforts and time (and often money, because old building owners have discovered that this can be a lucrative venture), sometimes you get a strange photo with a light anomaly or a whisper in an audio recording that almost sounds like your name.

Oh, I get it. I've done it many times and I'm sure several times in the next year, I'll be sitting somewhere in a cold, mold-infested basement talking to a rusty pipe and hoping that the readings on my K-2 EMF meter spike the moment after I ask a question. But I'm more interested in hunting ghost stories.

I've done enough research to understand that paranormal experiences aren't something that just happen all the time. They are impossible to replicate on demand. Glimpses of the truly fantastic are few and far between, but they've happened to enough people that I trust to know that there's something to it. I catalog those moments and combine them with boring old historical research to create haunted history walking tours.

I live in Wisconsin and when you grow up in the Midwest, it's easy to think of it as a boring place with not a lot of history. In the days before ghost hunting TV shows, my older sister and I would watch *That's Incredible!* or *Ripley's Believe it... or Not!* and it was always the paranormal stories that enthralled us the most. But they were always somewhere else.

And to be honest, Wisconsin doesn't have the glitz and glamour of the West Coast or the colonial centuries of the East Coast. And Winter seems to go on forever.

But just because no one was talking about it on TV doesn't mean it's not there. My sister was a schoolteacher and during her summer breaks, she started doing research in Milwaukee and created a tour there. I live seventy-five miles away in Madison and she helped me start a tour here, and we began what we now not-jokingly call "The Family Business". A decade later and now there are tours spread across several different cities and hundreds of miles.

Because there is plenty of fascinating history, intrigue, true crime, high drama, supernatural folklore, indigenous legends, ghost stories, cryptid sightings (like lake monsters and Bigfoot), UFO visitations, and occult activity right in our own backyard. It's haunted history tours that tap into that and when you see a city through the lens of the paranormal, you understand it in a brand new way. It's a chance to feel more powerfully connected to your own town or to feel a special relationship with a new place. There's weird no matter where you go and in Wisconsin that's doubly so.

There's a vacation town about halfway between Milwaukee and Chicago called Lake Geneva, right over the Illinois-Wisconsin border. It's most famous for being a playground for the wealthiest families in Chicago with massive summer homes built in the late Nineteenth Century, families with names like Wrigley, Maytag, Sears and Schwinn. When I was a kid, it was famous to me as the birthplace of *Dungeons & Dragons.* In fact, the GenCon gaming convention, which is a juggernaut in the tabletop-gaming industry, was started in Lake Geneva. They gave it the name Geneva Convention as a play on the rules of armed conflict, because before D&D existed, they were all playing wargames. It was the also about the only place in Wisconsin that you'd see Chicago Bears and Cubs flags flying alongside our beloved Green Bay Packers and Milwaukee Brewers banners because the sports bars were trying to cater to the Illinois market.

At the turn of the Twentieth Century though, Lake Geneva was also the home of America's finest sanitariums. I know what you're thinking. You've seen *Ghost Asylum* or you've seen Zak Bagans scream "Come at me, bro" while investigating Waverly Hills. You know what kind of hellholes these were. But these weren't some kind of dingy state-run facilities with tiny prison cell-like rooms. These were more like country clubs, like a rehab facility that Ben Affleck or Steven Tyler from Aerosmith would visit. Scenic lake views, green sprawling grounds—that's what these places were like. They were just as much of a high class hotel as a hospital.

These sanitariums were the brainchild of Oscar Augustus King, a groundbreaking physician who was a mixture of psychiatrist and neurologist. King even studied at the University of Vienna in Austria at almost the exact same time as the founder of psychoanalysis, Sigmund Freud (no idea what King thought of cigars, though.) He led the Wisconsin legislature to pass the first bills in the United States regulating mental health treatment and Wisconsin became the mental health capital of America. Indeed, no other state had as many sanitariums in the late Nineteenth Century. It wasn't just one big lobotomy nightmare like horror movies have led you to believe.

So, we've got a town with plenty of history and plenty of tourists, but no haunted history tour. Opportunity seemed to be knocking, so it was time to get to work.

After a few months of research in the local library, museum, and walking around talking to various businesses, I had a rough script. Through the magic of social media, I met two guides who were up for the job, Rita and Melinda. I met Rita because she had gone ghost hunting with her mother, who I interviewed while researching the tour. Her mom was in a local paranormal group that I had contacted because they had investigated some of the hotels downtown. Melinda came along on a practice tour Rita had run and had said she was interested. Melinda and her mother had recently curated an exhibit at the local museum called *Momento Mori*, that's Latin for a "reminder of death". I said we non-jokingly call it "The Family Business", didn't I?

Everyone is into this stuff when it's Halloween season. It's like how alcoholics call St. Patrick's Day "amateur night". To be into the paranormal all the time means you're inviting ridicule, particularly in modern times, where people have their teams drawn up politically. Ghosts are anathema to both atheist progressives and Christian fundamentalists. So when you find others in the weird tribe, you stick with them, and often it's your family members. They're judging you anyway, right? But they're stuck with you.

Anyway, we hadn't officially launched the tour yet because I was still trying to figure out a route through the downtown area that will take everyone near the most scenic parts while not being overly taxing physically, and also getting people somewhat close to their cars when the tour is over. Walking routes seem to work best in a circle and the whole thing usually works best if it's somewhere between 90 minutes and 2 hours. Think about how long you can make it without going to the bathroom during a movie. I don't know what I remember more about *Titanic,* the visually striking images of the majestic boat being torn asunder or the extra-large-soda-sized pressure on my bladder during the last hour of the film.

I took a walking tour in Anoka, Minnesota one time that lasted over three hours and we had to beg some teenager working at a Subway to use their restroom. I couldn't get my mind off the fact that my back teeth were floating for about 20 minutes of that tour and let's just say that it colored my opinion of the whole thing. Colored it yellow. So getting the route right is absolutely essential to the whole experience.

We wanted to launch our Lake Geneva tour by Memorial Day and we're walking through the temporary route on an incredibly beautiful day in early May. The lake is a dark blue under the sky's lighter hue and the temperature is perfect. In Wisconsin, we've got five reliably good months outdoors, and three of those months you are being hunted by mosquitoes, so you tend to appreciate the best days and remember them.

On the Main Street, there's a shop where Rita used to work and she mentioned that she had and some of the other employees had had a few strange experiences there. Now, this building is on the Wisconsin Historical Registry and was built by one of the pillars of Lake Geneva's early days, Frank Sherman Moore. He established a hardware store there in 1903 that would last through most of the Twentieth Century. Frank was a fairly diverse fellow, considered that not only was he a local hardware store owner, but he was the mayor of Lake Geneva in 1898 and served as postmaster for a decade. Frank was also a founding member of the Lake Geneva Knights of Pythias. Now, that's a sweet-sounding name for a secret society and I wish I could say that the Knights of Pythias were on par with the Freemasons for diabolical conspiracies secretly in charge of the world. Famous Pythians do include Presidents Warren G. Harding, William McKinley, and Franklin Delano Roosevelt, as well as jazz legend Louis Armstrong and Vice President Hubert Humphrey. Seems like they could be lizard people, but the most nefarious thing about the organization I could find about them was that you weren't supposed to drink.

And anytime you're talking about teetotalers, you're talking about Prohibition. Local Lake Genevans talk about boarded off tunnels underneath the downtown connecting all the buildings and going out near the lake and they're often rumored that they were getaway tunnels used by gangsters during the era when alcohol was illegal. The most famous mobsters during Prohibition were from Chicago, so you can bet that the nearest vacation destination had plenty of goombas running booze to the city. When the law comes knocking at the Speakeasy door, tunnels make sense. It's a much safer escape.

All over Wisconsin you hear stories of gangsters, in particular, Al Capone coming for a visit or spending the night at their inn or drinking at their bar. If Capone spent as much time vacationing in Wisconsin as people say he did, there is no way he would have had enough time to be a gangster kingpin in Chicago. However, you can see the entrance to underground tunnels in the basement of the store and Rita did find an extremely old gambling ledger full of numbers down there.

Now, when the shop had haunted stories from when she was working there, it was called Bouquets. Rita said they felt it was a feminine presence and then nicknamed the spirit, "Jennifer". That made me laugh because it was a shop that featured some Lake Geneva tourist-y type gifts, and in the early Twentieth Century, the nickname for the sea serpent people had seen in the lake was "Genny". Lake Geneva, Genny The Lake Monster, Jennifer the ghost... I was thinking that the locals could just try *a little harder* when it came to naming their spectres and cryptids.

Ghost Jennifer loved to cause mischief around the store, especially to customers who were rude and she didn't seem to like. Jennifer even almost made a lamp fall on a customer one time, but generally would just move around candles, turn lights on and off, and make little noises when no one else could have made them. However, the only physical manifestation that was seen was a male looking phantom who was seen on a security camera one time.

As far as males go, Frank Moore himself passed away on November 10th, 1936, but his building was a hardware store for decades and, while there were new owners, it was even called Moore Hardware. Who knows? Maybe it's Frank and not Jennifer who's annoyed with the rude customers? After all, the building was his and kept his name long after his death. Maybe he's still looking after it from beyond?

There is a stone header with the carving, "Paints Tinware F. S. Moore Hardware" that still sits above the Classical Revival columns in front of the structure and the whole thing is faced in Bedford Limestone. Bedford, Indiana bills itself as the "Limestone Capital of the World" and its stone has been used in famous places like The Empire State Building and The Pentagon. But it was extremely important in rebuilding the Windy City after the Great Chicago Fire and that's also the period where many of the buildings in Lake Geneva were constructed.

Among paranormal researchers, limestone buildings seem to have more ghost stories than others. Well, that could be because it was extremely popular in architecture in the late Nineteenth Century, so the buildings made with limestone seem really old. And really old buildings are, of course, the best breeding ground for ghost stories.

Another theory about why limestone is more paranormally sensitive is from Illinois author Timothy Yohe. Because limestone is partially made up of skeletal fragments of coral and other marine organisms, former living things, it might contain some residual living energy that spirits might be able to tap into. Because it's calcified bodies of sea life, he refers to it as "paranormal plankton".

And when it comes to haunting experiences, you have particular types of them. Sometimes, the ghost seems intelligent, like when you seem to be communicating with an entity through a Ouija Board (the gateway to Hell available at every toy store in the country.) Sometimes the ghost can't speak, but it reacts to things, like when a poltergeist throws a plate across the room. And sometimes, people just see a vision that seems like a replay of something that happened before, like when a Civil War soldier walks across an old battlefield. The phantom seems to walking through things and not paying any attention to the new world around him. The proper term for that is a "residual haunting".

There was a BBC movie from the early 1970s called *The Stone Tape* written by Nigel Kneale, the man who invented Professor Quatermass, one of Britain's great science fiction hero scientists. In the movie, a research team working in a eerie Victorian mansion postulates that ghosts and hauntings are like tape recordings, and that electrical mental impressions released during emotional or traumatic events can somehow be stored in rocks or walls and then will replay under certain conditions.

Because of the influence of the film, the idea of residual hauntings is often called the "Stone Tape" theory. So when you see that Civil War soldier, you're not seeing a ghost that refuses to step into the light, you're just seeing a recording of an event, like watching an old home movie that will only play on a very particular VCR. That's how old records work, you scrape a needle over a vinyl groove and you can hear the Beatles. What kind of material would work better as a "supernatural vinyl" than the "paranormal plankton" of limestone?

So, combine a historic limestone building with the

strange stories from the employees and we have enough for a stop on the tour. I had only been on the route in the night time and hadn't been in the store yet when it was open. As we were passing it walking through the route, Rita wondered aloud if the new management had any ghost stories. I was feeling hurried at the time to get back on the hour long drive to Madison to see my screaming 18-month old, so I was just about to say "let's find out another time", when Melinda opened the door and goes in.

Okay, I've done this before, so let's see what happens. I've had to start many conversations with the introductory phrase, "I know this is gonna sound weird" and then proceed to ask about the ghost stories. Paranormal experiences in particular often seem to get a strong reaction out of people and business owners, especially. They are either incredulous about the whole thing and have never had an experience or they're all in and their business is like when the containment unit burst in *Ghostbusters*, there's spirits oozing out of every crack in the wall. Either way, you're not getting a great story. If they don't believe, then you have to cross the place off your list. If they're into it *too much*, then you're left sorting out the good tales that have some history and credence from the BS that often follows the paranormal field.

When you're talking about ghosts and hauntings, I feel like we have a responsibility to be careful and stick to the "facts". Get the history right, get the details of the experience right, don't hypothesize about what you think the haunting is. Rule Number One for our tours is Don't Make Stuff Up.

In the movie *The Crow,* the bad guy Top Dollar (the wonderfully gravelly voiced Michael Wincott) says the line, "Childhood is over the moment you know you're gonna die." I remember the exact moment I realized that I was gonna die, and so was my sister and my mother and my father and all of my friends. I was six years old and I was reading this Charlie Brown children's encyclopedia. My parents got it free as a sample from a book store and it was the volume that covered the human body. In the book, it talks about death and how it happens to everyone. My parents didn't realize it, but that Charlie Brown encyclopedia was much more terrifying than any Stephen King or Clive Barker novel. After I understood the implications of what I was reading, I couldn't sleep the rest of the night. It was my first existential crisis, but everyone goes through one of those eventually. Mine just happened earlier than others.

People want to know there's another side. They hope they can see their loved ones again, they hope that they don't just end. That there is something besides oblivion waiting for them and the people they care about. It's easy to take advantage of, and I've fielded more than one call to our "Ghost Line" (Right, I know, it's a silly way to make people laugh to have them call our tour phone number) of someone distraught after the loss of their loved one, hoping that the human soul survives physical death.

When people are grieving and desperate for answers, they're easy to take advantage of. The frauds and hoaxers out there make everyone involved in the field look like immoral charlatans, willing to prey on the weakest among us. So many out there already think that anyone who is into the paranormal is a fool, do we want them to also think of us as shysters?

Hauntings can be really good for making money and some business owners understand this and some don't. There's a whole world of paranormal travel out there and people, like me, will pick one restaurant or bar or hotel over another because it has history and stories. If it's got too many stories, I'm wary of the place, because then there's often no scrutiny involved and you know it's probably just a marketing ploy. What makes a true-life ghost story exciting, to me at least, is its verisimilitude, not its outrageousness.

And often, it's the employees who tell the best stories. They're the ones that have the least to gain and the most to lose by telling their tales. No one is going to stake their reputation on something that didn't actually happen to them because they think they'll get a few more customers in their gift shop or a couple more patrons at the bar they wait tables at. While owners are often worried about losing their credibility or they're hoping to make extra money, their employees are usually just trying to get by.

So, it's a fairly unassuming shop full of designer plates, vases, soaps, and other types of home wares. It's the kind of pleasant-smelling store that usually bores weirdos like me to death, but it's perfect for frazzled moms to duck into during a vacation to get away from the street noise and the bustle of a daytime downtown right off the lake. By the time I got in there, my guide had already started talking to the lady working behind the register.

She was in her forties, auburn hair running to her shoulders, and she had a friendly smile for us, even as I overheard her telling my guide that she had never experienced anything like *that* in the store. And of course, she doesn't believe in that stuff anyway, because she's Catholic.

That's not the first time I've heard that. I grew up in the Church, in the kind of family that didn't eat meat on Fridays and went to Mass every Sunday (and you better believe we didn't miss a Holy Day of Obligation) and I'll tell ya, I don't remember ever talking about ghosts. I did ask a priest about the Ouija Board because I thought it was totally cool, but he said that we weren't supposed to try and "conjure" the dead. So, that means that visits to mediums and psychics are out too, I guess.

I'm not gonna talk about the "Holy Ghost" because that's just supposed to be the spirit of faith and not some disembodied soul running around. But the Church teaches about "The Communion of Saints", and it's a phrase we used to repeat that we believed in during the Apostle's Creed every week. The Communion of Saints is the idea that every member of the Church, living or deceased, is connected to each other through

"The Mystical Body of Christ" (which sounds a lot cooler in its Latin form, *Mystici corporis Christi*). They teach that we're actually connected to the dead except for the souls that are damned to Hell.

And don't forget about Purgatory. There's actually a place where the dead go when they're not bad enough for Hell or good enough for Heaven. The Church even says that sometimes the souls will have to make up for their naughty deeds in Purgatory and can appear on Earth before they can go to Heaven. So, boom. There's officially plenty of room for actual ghosts (not just demons masquerading as ghosts) in Catholicism. It just has to be part of God's will. And I guess if you're religious, everything is God's will anyway. So, next time a Catholic tells you that ghosts are a no-go, you can hit them with the one-two punch of Purgatory and the Communion of Saints.

I wasn't about to engage in theological fisticuffs with this nice lady in the store, though. I was already running late and I wanted to make this visit as short as possible. She said she's never had any experiences there at all and didn't believe in that kind of stuff, to boot. That's good enough for me.

But Rita, who used to work there, mentioned to the woman that she used to be employed in the store and was hoping we could take a look around in the basement. Since there was no one else in the place, the lady said that's completely fine and offered to take us down there. I thought, that's great anyway, because it'll help me to visualize the location where they found the gambling notebook while rewriting the story for the tour.

We went down the stairs cheerfully and the lady was being perfectly lovely about everything. It was the early afternoon, a beautiful sunny day at the end of Spring. This was the time of year in the Midwest where everyone is naturally in a good mood. We were laughing and joking a bit as I took in the surroundings. Not too musty, it had a got a cement floor at least (there are plenty of old buildings where the basement has a dirt floor.) Random items from the store filled the shelves and were placed strategically across the ground. There were no basement windows or anything, so the light came from a few bulbs with pullchains, but it wasn't too dark or dim or particularly spooky. I was hoping that Ghost Jennifer might come jumping out at us from a hidden corner, but she was nowhere to be found. The walls were old and of course, it felt like it had been around for a century, but that's pretty standard for the area.

All in all, a regular old basement with some nooks and crannies. There is a semi-crumbled entrance to what looks like could have been an underground tunnel system, but it seems to have been filled in, which makes sense because that could be a flooding nightmare. My guide showed me where she found the gambling notebook as we crossed the floor.

As we got to a slightly less well-lit area and it seemed like the basement went on for awhile in the dark, I noticed there's a section where there were some studs up for a side storage area that seemed like walls were never put up. Or the walls had been taken down. Either way, there was nothing too exciting about it that I could tell, just an area where the construction remained unfinished in either build up or tear down. Not strange because it was probably on the to-do list of the owners as something to get around to eventually.

As we were walking, the lady from the store was talking happily. "Here's where we keep the extra inventory and I've been down here alone plenty of times. I've never seen or felt anything..." And her voice trailed off as we got closer to the unfinished storage area. She was at my back and I wasn't paying that much attention to her because I didn't think she had anything for us. Because she suddenly stopped talking, we all turned around to her.

Her eyes were watering and she continued weakly, "There's just something about this corner, I just..." And she stopped again. Her eyes teared up more heavily and she started crying in front of us, openly. Real weeping, like she was watching *Titanic* and it just got to the part where Leonardo DiCaprio is about to let go of Kate Winslet's hands on the raft. She was completely overcome with emotion. Melinda, the one who had rushed in in the first place, said, "It's the little girl, isn't it?"

She continued, "You lost someone like the little girl. The little girl that's still here, in that room over there, in the corner." She pointed to the unfinished storage area. "That's why she's reaching out to you." The woman weakly nodded through her tears. There was an intense energy in the room, a static electricity that I could feel, like when you finally get to the point in an argument where something has been said that can't be unsaid. There was an atmosphere in the basement and it changed. I knew that something was happening to these women, but I couldn't see it. They embraced in a kind of hug and turned around and walked back towards the stairs.

I looked over at the corner, and of course, I didn't see any shadows or ghosts. I'm about as psychically sensitive as a callous, but the natural sympathy when you see someone crying is overwhelming. To my eyes, I just saw a corner and an unfinished storage closet. But my breath was taken away by witnessing this woman who didn't believe in ghosts and steadfastly insist that she had zero paranormal experiences in this place *except* for the corner of the basement that makes her sob inexplicably.

So, we walked back to the stairs slowly and you could hear some people chatting. Instead of just us eccentrics, there were actual customers in the store. The woman wiped her eyes, steadied herself, put on her best smile, and went back upstairs to talk to them and hopefully make a sale. We thanked her for her time, she nodded, got to the real consumers, and we walked out into the sunlight.

At that point, I was still a little dazed by what happened. Serious people who are non-believers do not have a paranormal crying fit in front of complete strangers. But that lady just did. That's when Melinda happened to mention that she's "sensitive" and she detected the presence of the little girl who was in that corner. It wasn't the lady's little girl, but the spirit was attracted to the shopkeeper because she had lost a child close to her.

Okay, well I can't vouch for any of that, but I did just witness something extraordinary. I told Melinda that her gifts are awesome, however, I don't know that we want to be in the business of connecting people to their dead relatives. We do haunted history, not séances. But of course, if she gets any psychic messages that we can investigate for new tour stops, I'm all in.

We all looked at each other in amazement for a minute, kinda processing the whole thing, but I was still in a hurry. There were only a couple of tour stops left and we walked through them quickly. After all, everything felt anticlimactic after that. We talked about the tour launch and I raced back on the hour drive to Madison. I tried to tell my wife about it, but it was hard to get the words in over the screaming baby and it must have seemed like a crazy story, and I didn't even write any of it down until the next day.

Since then, we've run hundreds of tours now in Lake Geneva. We've told that story at several different conferences and I still have no idea what compelled that woman to break down in front of us. There was something non-physical in that basement that had the ability to evoke some powerful emotions. Could it be mold or some fungus playing with our brain chemistry? Sure. Could Melinda and the shopkeeper have concocted the whole thing in the few moments before Rita and I followed her inside? Possibly. Could everyone involved be susceptible to this kind of suggestion because we had it on our minds? Absolutely.

Order Your Books Today!

Book	Price	Amount	Total
Subscription to parABnormal			
One Year	$34.00		
Two Year	$60.00		
Herd Lord by Beth Hudson	$5.99		
Judas: America Bound by Lanegan Bicchieri With P.H. Glass	$5.95		
Etched in Fire by Beth Hudson	$26.99		
Tidings of Madness and Joy by Bill Otto	$11.00		
		Subtotal	$
		Shipping	
		1 book	$3.80
		2 books	$4.35
		3 books	$4.90
		4 or more books	$6.00
		Final Total	$

Name: ____

Address: ____

City: ____

State: ____

Zip: ____

Phone: ____

Date: ____

Checks or money orders need to be made out to Alban Lake Publishing.

For Credit Card Orders:

Card #: ____

Exp. Date: _______________________________________

Security Code: ___________________________________

Date: ____

Signature: _______________________________________

Alban Lake Publishing
P.O. Box 141
Colo, IA 50056-014
515-357-8910 (texts welcome)
albanlake@yahoo.com
Website: www.albanlakepublishing.com